"Sarah, you need to think of the baby. Even if you're not worried about your own safety."

Sarah's idea of tall, dark and handsome had shifted.

And now it was somewhere at tall, blue-eyed and built to wrap around her just so. She fit into the circle of Cooper Bellamy's arms the way a diamond solitaire fit into its setting. Aligned against his chest, tucked beneath his chin, with his broad shoulders to lean into. His long arms to shield her and her baby from any trouble the outside world tried to throw at her.

She could feel things all right. Maybe her brother had been right to steer her away from a relationship with Coop.

But she couldn't resist.

P9-ELS-043

JULIE MILLER

NINE-MONTH PROTECTOR

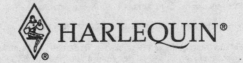

HARLEQUIN®

TORONTO • NEW YORK • LONDON
AMSTERDAM • PARIS • SYDNEY • HAMBURG
STOCKHOLM • ATHENS • TOKYO • MILAN • MADRID
PRAGUE • WARSAW • BUDAPEST • AUCKLAND

If you purchased this book without a cover you should be aware
that this book is stolen property. It was reported as "unsold and
destroyed" to the publisher, and neither the author nor the
publisher has received any payment for this "stripped book."

For Taz.

I've dedicated books to my writers' group before, but I
especially want to thank Sue Baumann, who took over
as president from me in 2006, and has been a wonderful,
inspirational leader for our group. She's a woman with
heart, talent and a clever sense of humor. I appreciate
your leadership, support and friendship, and, of course—
the wet noodles and candy corn pumpkins. Thanks.

ISBN-13: 978-0-373-69282-8
ISBN-10:   0-373-69282-X

NINE-MONTH PROTECTOR

Copyright © 2007 by Julie Miller

All rights reserved. Except for use in any review, the reproduction or
utilization of this work in whole or in part in any form by any electronic,
mechanical or other means, now known or hereafter invented, including
xerography, photocopying and recording, or in any information storage
or retrieval system, is forbidden without the written permission of the
publisher, Harlequin Enterprises Limited, 225 Duncan Mill Road,
Don Mills, Ontario, Canada M3B 3K9.

This is a work of fiction. Names, characters, places and incidents are
either the product of the author's imagination or are used fictitiously,
and any resemblance to actual persons, living or dead, business
establishments, events or locales is entirely coincidental.

This edition published by arrangement with Harlequin Books S.A.

® and ™ are trademarks of the publisher. Trademarks indicated with
® are registered in the United States Patent and Trademark Office, the
Canadian Trade Marks Office and in other countries.

www.eHarlequin.com

Printed in U.S.A.

ABOUT THE AUTHOR

Julie Miller attributes her passion for writing romance to shyness and all those fairy tales she read growing up. Encouragement from her family to write down all those feelings she couldn't express became a love for the written word. She gets continued support from her fellow members of the Prairieland Romance Writers, where she serves as the resident "grammar goddess." This award-winning author and teacher has published several paranormal romances. Inspired by the likes of Agatha Christie and Encyclopedia Brown, Ms. Miller believes the only thing better than a good mystery is a good romance.

Born and raised in Missouri, she now lives in Nebraska with her husband, son and smiling guard dog, Maxie. Write to Julie at P.O. Box 5162, Grand Island, NE 68802-5162.

Books by Julie Miller

*The Taylor Clan
**The Precinct
†The Precinct: Vice Squad

CAST OF CHARACTERS

Cooper Bellamy—This KCPD detective has always been the backup, but his unresolved feelings for his partner's sister force him to take the lead when her life is threatened.

Sarah Cartwright—Mild-mannered schoolteacher. Mom-to-be. Murder witness. Finding out the truth about her unborn baby's father might be the one thing that could save her life.

Seth Cartwright—When he can't be there to keep his sister safe, there's no one he'd trust with the job more than his partner, Coop. As long as Coop keeps his hands to himself.

Theodore Wolfe—London-born mob boss with endless resources and connections to draw upon anywhere in the world.

Shaw McDonough—Hit man with a hidden agenda.

Sandoval—A young cop.

Uncle Walt—He knows a little about a lot of things.

Kenny Sterling—He rents cabins, leads fishing trips and shoots trespassers.

John Kincaid—Captain of the Major Case Squad task force Cooper and Seth work for. Soon-to-be deputy Commissioner of KCPD.

Chapter One

Sarah Cartwright ran into the posh gold-and-porcelain appointments of Teddy Wolfe's bathroom and puked.

She knelt in front of the commode, clutching her stomach and grinding her knuckles against her mouth until the worst of the humiliation had passed.

What an idiot. What an idiot!

"Sarah?" The millionaire owner of the Riverboat Casino rapped on the door. "Will you be all right?"

Only if the tile floor opened up and swallowed her whole.

Her mouth opened to form words, but she couldn't speak. What was there to say after what she'd just learned? After what she'd just done? Was there anything she could say that could make this whole evening go away?

She could hear Teddy outside the door, getting dressed. Fine leather creaked—a belt? His Italian oxfords? The holster and Beretta she'd seen lying on his desk?

She'd known he wasn't the average sort of sweet and dependable guy she usually dated. That air of danger about him, that unpredictability, had been what had made him seem so exciting in the first place. She should have known she was out of her league. Out of her depth. Out of her mind when she'd started trading phone calls and had accepted this date with him.

"Well," he continued in that suave British accent that she'd foolishly fallen for. "Take as long as you need. Make use of any of the facilities in my suite. Order room service from the restaurant or a bottle of champagne from the bar. But you'll have to enjoy the bubbly by yourself. I have some business to attend to. My people will take care of you."

She heard the whisper of silk sliding against silk outside the door as he continued to dress. Or maybe that was the smooth sound of careless, heartless—meaningless—seduction that she'd succumbed to like the naive, wide-eyed homebody she was. Her stomach churned again and she leaned forward.

After growing up the daughter of Austin Cartwright, she'd always fancied herself so smart about the world. But how could she not have seen this coming? Had she really felt so lonesome? So bored with her life? So left behind in the relationship world, after marrying off friend after friend—and even her own mother—that she'd refused to see the obvious?

She couldn't call it rape. She'd been a willing participant. It had been fun and daring, and she'd had no desire to say no.

She'd been exactly the exciting new woman she wanted to be. It was the adventurous relationship she'd wanted to have.

But she hadn't known. If only she had known.

"Sarah?" Teddy sounded impatient now, irritated with her silence. His evening hadn't turned out the way he'd planned, either. He probably expected her to thank him.

"I'm fine," she squeaked out on a whisper. She cleared her throat and reached for one of the crystal glasses on the counter. She pulled herself to her feet, filled the glass with cold water and took a swallow before repeating in a louder, stronger voice. "I'm fine."

It was a lie, but it didn't matter. That was all Teddy wanted to hear. Teddy with the smooth line and smoother kisses. Teddy with the money. Teddy with the gun. Teddy with the awful, awful words.

"You can tell your father we're square."

"What?" Not exactly the romantic pillow talk she'd expected after their first time together. Sarah pushed herself up on her elbows and pulled the straps of her sundress back onto her shoulders while Teddy disposed of their protection, stood and zipped his pants.

"I'll consider his debt paid in full. For now. Until the next time he loses more than he can afford to."

Whatever sense of adventure had driven her to risk her heart so quickly faded in a haze of confusion. *"What are you talking about?"*

"The two-hundred-and-sixty grand Austin owes me. Owed me. There's no need to worry about your father now. I'll make sure nothing happens to him." Teddy was speaking so matter-of-factly, like they'd just conducted a business transaction instead of an impulsive makeout session on the leather couch in his private suite above the casino. He picked up his shirt and leaned over to kiss

her. *"That was just what I needed. Thank you for the lovely evening."*

Oh, no. No.

"Was my father in danger?" What had Austin gotten himself into this time? Her stomach twisted into knots. *"And I...? This was just...?"*

Sarah couldn't even bring herself to say the horrible thing she'd just done. Her own father had put a price on her head.

She grabbed her shoes and her purse and dashed into the bathroom, locking the door, locking out the nightmarish mistake she'd just made.

"Yes, well, it's been fun, hasn't it?" Teddy was moving outside the door, ready to leave. "We'll have to do this again sometime."

Sarah gripped the edge of the sink. *I don't think so. Never.*

Teddy's voice grew louder as he leaned against the bathroom door. "Austin raised a gem in spite of himself. Good night."

After the outside door to the suite closed, Sarah splashed some of the cold water on her face and neck. She stared at her reflection in the light-studded mirror. She didn't look any different—straight blond hair, slightly askew around her face. Big green eyes framed by the tiny lines of worry she'd earned in her twenty-seven years. She was as frustratingly petite and tomboyishly slim as she'd always been.

But there was something different about her. Something hollow in her expression. A weariness of the world that came from a lesson learned too late.

"I need to get out of here."

Before something so useless as tears could take hold, Sarah scrubbed her face clean, zipped up the back of her dress and fastened her strappy sandals around her ankles. She fished her keys from her purse, put her ear to the door to make sure she was alone and pushed it open.

"Go home," she advised herself. "Go home, regroup, pretend this never happened. No, call Dad and tell him he and I are done." She crossed the Persian rug with a more purposeful stride. "There's not a damn thing he can say to make this one right."

Austin Cartwright was a sick man. His gambling addiction had cost the family plenty over the years. College funds, the dissolution of her parents' marriage, a deep rift between father and brother. Trust.

Still she'd persevered. Austin Cartwright was her daddy. The man who'd carried her on his shoulders as a little girl. The man who'd taught her how to fish, how to hammer a nail, how to keep a box score at a baseball game. He'd taught her how to have fun. Sarah remembered having fun when she was little. She'd had fun without second-guessing the motive behind an activity, without doubting the sincerity behind the companionship.

Long after her mother had left Austin to protect her son and daughter from his illness and the resulting moods and dangers, long after she'd learned that gambling was an addiction—not unlike drug or alcohol abuse—and that it diminished her father's reliability and tainted his love, she'd tried to help him. Sarah had tried to keep him in Gamblers Anonymous, tried to steer him away from the casino he'd practically rebuilt with his own hands. She'd tried to be patient, tried to listen, tried to be tough with her affection. She'd continued to be there for a man who was difficult to love.

But this was too much.

This was the ultimate betrayal.

This one she couldn't forgive.

And she'd been too blinded by her need to crash out and take a break from the heavy responsibilities of her devotion to even see it coming.

Her father had sold her to repay a gambling debt.

Sarah Cartwright knew exactly what she was worth to her father now. Two-hundred-and-sixty-thousand dollars and a clean slate to start betting the odds all over again.

"Yeah, Dad, we're done. I can't forgive you this—"

She jumped as someone pounded on the outside door. "Teddy? Teddy!"

The woman's shrill voice stopped Sarah in her tracks. *Damn.* Her escape was cut off. No way could she handle a confrontation right now. No way did she even want to be seen anywhere near Teddy's suite.

"I know you have another woman in there. It's that slut…"

But Sarah was already running in the opposite direction. A suite of rooms had to have another exit, didn't it? A back door? A service elevator? A dumbwaiter? Hell, she'd open a window and dive into the Missouri River at the base of the floating casino if that were the only way to get out of this humiliating predicament without being seen.

Sarah opened a door with shuttered panels. Walk-in

closet. She closed it and moved on. She found a connecting door with a dead bolt and turned the lock. A matching door greeted her on the other side. The angry, unhappy woman's voice faded into a terse, hushed conversation with someone else outside in the hall. Sarah didn't try to make out any words or identify the speakers; she was focused on her escape.

Once the second bolt slid aside, she pushed open the door and discovered a second suite, mirroring the office and living quarters of Teddy's rooms. There was a second bathroom, a second closet, a second office. That meant there'd be a matching exit. Sarah ran to it.

"Don't throw yourself at him." A man's voice, deeper than Teddy's but tinged with the same articulate accent, spoke in soothing tones outside the door. "There's a difference between passion and possession."

Damn! How crowded could this supposedly private wing be at three in the morning?

Sarah backpedaled, looking for another option. Any option.

The man was talking to a woman out in the hall. The same woman who had shouted at the other door. Her anger spent, the woman sniffed back tears. "But I love him. You know, the money doesn't really matter. I just want him… I want us to be a family."

"Don't make it so easy for him to have you. Teddy likes the thrill of the chase."

A key scraped inside the door lock. Sarah froze. They were coming inside!

Run.

Where?

Sarah's heart hammered in her chest. She swept her gaze back and forth. Sofa. Door. Desk. Toilet. Her feet itched to go one direction but her brain argued another route would be safer.

Think.

"But Mr. McDonough," the woman pleaded, apparently stopping the man's hand on the doorknob. "I told him the truth. He said he loved me. But tonight I saw him with…"

Step by silent step, Sarah retreated. She did not want to be caught here. Did not want to have to explain to anyone why she was in Teddy's suite. Being an invited guest sounded like a lousy excuse right about now. And being the bartered payoff for her father's debt…? Could these people take one look at her and guess how she'd been duped? Would they laugh at her? Spread rumors? *Blame* her? How could she possibly defend herself? The woman outside was talking about *love*. And she'd… She'd…

The lock snapped open. Oh, hell. Sarah swung open the closet door and ducked inside. She closed the door behind her and hunkered down behind a row of tobacco-scented suits, clinging to the back wall of the closet, merging with the shadows, holding her breath in the darkness as the outside door opened and the couple came into the suite.

Their voices became clear, their actions easier to judge by the sounds they made. The woman was clearly upset. The man handed her a tissue or handkerchief and offered to pour her a drink. The woman sat on the leather couch. "Just water, thanks."

The man crossed to the connecting doors between the suites and paused, as though wondering why they'd been left open. Sarah heard a click and a grate as he closed and locked the connecting doors. Her stomach tumbled. She curled her arms around her bent knees and forced herself to breathe evenly, silently, through her open mouth. She was trapped.

"There." The man crossed back into the room. "I told you Teddy was gone. There's no other woman here for you to fret about."

Sarah's cheeks heated with embarrassment, then grew cold as she listened to more of the sad repercussions of her uncharacteristically impulsive actions.

"I'm not making this up, you know," the woman went on. "I really am pregnant."

The sofa creaked again. He was sitting beside her. Comforting her? "So you're carrying the heir to the Wolfe International fortune?"

"I don't think of it like that. To me, it's just Teddy's baby."

Teddy had fathered a baby? And he'd put the moves on Sarah? *"That was just what I needed."*

Creep. Bastard. Sarah seethed in silence.

"Dawn, you understand that Teddy's father is very traditional in a number of ways, despite his innovative business ideas. Family means as much to him as his reputation does. He'd expect Teddy to marry you. He'd want you and Teddy to move back to London."

"But that's what I want." The woman named Dawn sniffed, sounding hopeful. "I mean, I could live in London or anywhere he wants. I know he doesn't want to be tied down, and he has so many responsibilities here at the casino—"

"The casino can run just fine without him. Better, in fact."

"Better? What do you mean?"

Mr. McDonough of the deep accent and solicitous voice scoffed. It was a derisive sound, full of contempt. But was it meant for Dawn? Or for Teddy? "Fathering a grandchild for Mr. Wolfe would be the one thing Teddy could do to get back in his father's good graces."

Dawn sniffed. "What are you talking about?"

"Here. Rest your head. Go on, lie down." The man named McDonough soothed away the concerns his hushed aside had brought on. "I'll have a talk with Teddy. He's thirty years old. He needs to grow up one day. I'm sure he has feelings for you." He was consoling her, holding her perhaps, tucking her in to sleep off her distress. If only Teddy had such a heart. If only her father could remember what real caring meant. "I'll take care of everything," he promised. "You just leave it all up to me."

The sofa creaked.

"What are you doing? What is—?"

Thwap. Thwap.

Sarah lurched inside her sandals. She pressed her hand tightly over her mouth to keep from crying out.

She knew that sound.

Gunshots. Muffled by a suppressor, but no less distinct.

Her mother was a cop. Commissioner of KCPD.

Her brother was a cop. Used to be, at any rate.

Her brother's best friend and half the people she knew were cops. She'd been around guns all her adult life.

Someone had been shot.

It was way too quiet in the other room. The crying had stopped.

Sarah's pulse throbbed in her ears, making it difficult to hear the words from the other room as the weight shifted on the sofa. "You were a damned inconvenience, Dawn. But I think now you'll serve my purpose very well."

When Sarah heard footsteps tapping over the tile floor in the bathroom—a whole half a room away—she scrambled across the closet and knelt on her hands and knees, peering through the slats at the door.

Oh, God. Oh, my God.

Dawn, a pretty woman she'd seen working in the casino on previous visits, lay across the couch, her head nestled against a pillow, her arm dangling to the floor. The long, blond hair at her temple was matting with sticky crimson.

The man she'd sought comfort from—Mr. McDonough—strode back into the room. Sarah flinched, instinctively backing away from the threat carrying a gun in his hand. But still she watched.

He was older than Teddy, though not yet her father's age. McDonough was well dressed, well groomed with super-short hair and dark, nearly black eyes she would never forget.

Those cold eyes showed no emotion whatsoever as he unscrewed the suppressor from his gun, holstered the weapon and knelt beside Dawn's body—and the infant inside her who would now die as well. "There will be no grandchild, dear. Teddy's been a disappointment to his father for a long time. I can't have you changing that."

He wrapped a towel around Dawn's head and the

pillow. Then he pulled out a roll of kitchen plastic from the wet bar and wrapped it around her body from head to toe, lifting and dropping the dead woman as though she were a rag doll instead of someone's daughter or lover or sister—or mother.

Sarah wanted to curl up into a ball. She wanted to curse his cruelty. She wanted to cry out.

But all she could do was hold herself perfectly still, down on her hands and knees, setting aside the humiliation of her evening and swallowing her shock and horror. She silently watched McDonough wrap the plastic mummy of Dawn's body in one of the rugs. He called maintenance for a cart and rolled her out the door like so much trash.

Nearly an hour passed before Sarah could move again. Her fingers were numb from their tight grip in the carpeting; her skin was ice-cold. She finally breathed her first decent breath and crawled out of the closet.

What the hell was she supposed to do now?

Hide? Find Teddy? Warn him of McDonough's treachery? Ask about Dawn? Run for her life before McDonough came back and discovered her here?

She'd been hoping she could just walk away from the nightmarish mistake of her night with Teddy Wolfe. Bury her head in the sand and nurse her ego alone in the privacy of her apartment for a few days.

But all that had changed.

Sarah Cartwright might have trained to be a fourth-grade teacher instead of a woman of adventure, but the blood of law enforcement—of justice and honor and doing the right thing even when it was tough—ran in her veins.

Wanting to put some distance between her and McDonough, she hurried across the casino's deserted parking lot, praying the dark of night would cover her escape. She climbed into her car and locked herself inside. Glancing in the rearview mirror to make sure no one was following her, she pulled onto the street heading toward home. Then, she finally picked up her cell phone and dialed 9-1-1.

She knew the drill, knew what she had to do.

"Kansas City 9-1-1 Emergency Assistance Center. How may I direct your call?"

Sarah swallowed hard. "I need to report a murder."

"I JUST NEED YOU TO CHECK on her for me, okay? I know you didn't sign on for babysitting duty, but it'd be a load off my mind."

Detective Cooper Bellamy listened to his partner's request, already pulling a clean T-shirt from his drawer and tucking it into the jeans he'd donned as soon as his phone had rung in the middle of the night. Though he'd be dressed and on the job before this conversation was done, he had to put up some kind of argument when Seth Cartwright had called to tell him he was worried about his twin sister's safety.

"I'm sure it's in the fine print somewhere, buddy." He could almost hear the hitch in Seth's *Dragnet*-serious voice as Coop harassed him into a relieved harumph. "I provide intel. Report to the chief. Save your ass. Babysit your sister. I do it all."

"You're a god among men, Coop." Seth could dish it out as well as he could take it.

"I keep tellin' you that."

Coop told a lot of jokes. Laughter had always been his antidote for dealing with the crap that life threw at a man. If he didn't admit to the pain, then he didn't have to feel it. If no one saw him hurting, then they'd trust that he was strong. They'd find strength in his confidence. Believe in his abilities. He never wanted to look into a loved-one's eyes and see that worry, that fear—that lack of faith in him again.

He'd never have to look into his partner's eyes and see any doubt that he'd come through for him.

Coop slipped his holster straps over his shoulders and unlocked the Glock from his bedside table. Trust was everything between cops. Especially when one was working a dangerous undercover assignment, and *he* was the man assigned to ghost him. Coop was the detective whose job it was to take care of everything else—including checking on wayward family members—so that the inside man didn't have to risk blowing his cover and could concentrate on getting the evidence and staying alive.

Cooper and Seth had been recruited from the Fourth Precinct to serve on a special vice squad task force. On this assignment, Seth had infiltrated Wolfe International—the corporate front for a mob family putting down roots in Kansas City. Seth had the trust of the Wolfe family in his back pocket.

And Coop had Seth's.

But if Seth had any inkling that Coop's teasing flirtations with his pretty, petite sister had a ring of real longing in them, then—partner or not—Coop would be the last person Seth would call on to help.

An appreciative wolf whistle at seeing Sarah Cartwright in a dress for the first time had been enough for Seth to jump his case.

"If you weren't my partner, my best friend... If my life wasn't still in your hands for the next few days, I'd lay you flat out."

Coop raised his hands in surrender. "Hey, I'm just being an observant detective. So what if your twin sister puts on a little lipstick? I still think of her as the left-fielder who ran down that final out in our co-ed softball game against the fire department last summer. Hitting on your sister is a no-no. I get that."

"That's nonnegotiable, Coop."

"Understood."

Sure. Yeah. His brain understood. He understood even better than Seth himself that he wasn't the man for Sarah. Not in his wildest dreams could he make something work with a sweet, wholesome girl like her. Not for long. She'd want kids, roots, picket fences... He couldn't give her that. She deserved a better man. A whole man.

But sometimes the eye...the hormones...other things deep inside him...didn't always follow the logic.

So he could look. Maybe he could even lust a little. But he couldn't do anything about it. And he damn straight couldn't tell his partner what a hottie his sister was.

He had to be her big brother, too.

Coop checked his clip, holstered his gun and hooked his badge over his belt before heading to the front door. On the way out, he picked up his blue KCPD ball cap and pulled it on over his clean-shaven head. "Is she at home?"

"That's the million-dollar question. I can't find her.

She's turned off her cell, and all I get at her apartment is the damn answering machine."

"Sarah's a big girl, Seth," Coop tried to reason, climbing into his truck. He started the engine, not particularly thrilled by one obvious possibility. "Maybe she's on a date."

"At three in the morning?"

Um, earth to Seth. Big green eyes? Gorgeous smile? Just because Sarah was pint-sized and favored running shoes over stiletto heels didn't mean any man worth his salt wouldn't notice her. "You've never stayed up late when you were out with a woman you liked?"

"This isn't about me. You know Sarah and I are cut from different cloth. *I'm* the evil twin. She's the reliable one. She doesn't do wild and crazy and stay out all night."

Coop shook his head at the self-deprecating comment. He didn't know whether to remind Seth that he had proven himself one of the good guys time and again, or explain that *reliable* didn't necessarily mean stick-in-the-mud. If Sarah wanted to go out and party all night, she had the right. She was on summer vacation, after all. It wasn't as though she had to get up and teach in the morning.

Instead of arguing either point, Coop turned on the AC and adjusted the truck cab's interior to combat the muggy summer night outside. His job was to take care of Seth's needs outside of his assignment, not beat some sense into his stubborn head. It was time he went to work. "Has Sarah been seeing anyone? Can you give me the names of some friends I can call?"

"You know I haven't been able to keep in touch with

her like I should. Hell, I don't even know if Mom and Eli are back from their honeymoon yet." He could hear Seth's frustration. "Mom" was KCPD Commissioner Shauna Cartwright-Masterson, and Eli Masterson was her new husband—an investigator with the D.A.'s office. "All I know is I've seen Sarah at the casino on and off the past couple of weeks. Now tonight, I can't find her. I can't find my dad, either. But I figure whatever trouble he's gotten into, he deserves it."

Growing up in the Cartwright household couldn't have been easy with an absent father whose gambling addiction seemed to cause trouble whenever he did try to be a part of his family's lives. Coop knew all about stepping in to fill a father's place. He'd lost his own dad, a Marine Corps captain, during the first Gulf War, and had helped his mom raise his three younger siblings. Though Austin Cartwright was still alive and kicking, Seth had assumed a similar role. He might be only twelve minutes older than his sister, but Seth took his big-brother role very seriously.

But if Seth was 27, then so was Sarah. One of these days, he was going to have to accept that. "Like I said, she's a big girl."

"I just need to know she's all right," Seth insisted. He recited the address, and Coop jotted down the directions. "Just check on her for me, okay? Everything's about to blow here. It's too dangerous. And if Wolfe finds out I'm still workin' for KCPD…"

He didn't have to finish how deadly those repercussions could be to anyone Seth cared about.

Coop backed into the street and headed across town

toward Sarah's apartment, feeling an increased sense of urgency. "Talk to me, buddy. Tell me exactly what the situation is."

Seth gave Cooper a concise rundown of the night's events at the Riverboat Casino—the suspected front for Wolfe International's money-laundering activities. There'd been a big poker tournament there that night, and Seth believed he had proof of how Teddy Wolfe was filtering drug money through the tournament records and payouts. More than that, a Wolfe enforcer that they knew was good for at least one murder had attacked two women—one of them a leggy reporter named Rebecca Page. She was running some kind of investigation on her own, and she had Seth's focus and libido all twisted up into knots. Coop suspected his partner's feelings for the reporter ran a lot deeper than even Seth would admit.

And somehow, while Seth was focused on protecting Rebecca and making his case against the Wolfes, Sarah Cartwright had wandered into the mess. She'd been paying several visits to the casino over the past couple of weeks. Seth had monitored her comings and goings as best he could without drawing attention to the personal connection between them. But tonight, with evidence falling into place, a killer to subdue and a crime scene to secure, Seth had lost track of his sister.

"It could be nothing," Seth continued. "But I don't want to take any chances. I have to get to the hospital."

"You hurt?"

"Nah."

"Rebecca?"

"Not as badly as the other woman. But I want to

make sure Bec has a doctor look at her injuries. You should have seen her, Coop. You should have heard her telling him where to stick it. Remind me never to pick a fight with her." There was an uncharacteristic catch in his voice. It was part admiration, part fear. "I just need to know she's okay."

As much as he needed to know his sister was okay, too.

"Go." Coop wasn't about to fail him now. "You take care of Rebecca. I'll track down Sarah for you."

"Keep her safe."

"I'll keep her safe," Coop promised.

He hung up and merged into the light traffic on I-70 that would take him into the heart of downtown Kansas City, just a few blocks south of Sarah's restored loft in the City Market district. It was the most sensible place to start. If he discovered anything more sinister than Sarah's phone being left off the hook so she could get a good night's sleep, then he'd be at the starting point to retrace her steps for the night.

Cooper Bellamy's job was to ghost his partner. If that backup meant standing in as big brother while Seth dealt with trouble at the casino, then so be it.

He made it to Sarah's neighborhood in twenty minutes. It took him another five to locate the converted warehouse and connected parking garage Seth had described. Coop circled the garage until he found her car, then pulled up beside it and got out. He laid a hand on the hood of her sporty Ford Focus. Still warm. So the prodigal sister *had* been out on the town until the wee hours of the morning.

"Good for you, kid." She deserved to have a little fun

without reporting every move to Seth. Chances were she'd gone straight to bed, and checking on her now would only wake her. Still, a promise was a promise. For Seth's peace of mind—and, therefore, his own—Coop needed to see Sarah Cartwright with his own eyes so he could report that she was okay. He crossed through the glassed-in walkway over the street to the former warehouse-turned-apartment building.

The lobby here on the second floor was just as empty and quiet as the closed architectural firm on the first floor below him. Bypassing the noise of the 1930s-era elevator, Coop hit the stairs and climbed the two flights to Sarah's floor.

By the time he reached the tomblike silence of the fourth floor, Coop felt the first measure of suspicion. Why *was* it so quiet in Sarah's building? There were plenty of vehicles in the parking garage to account for several of the apartments in this block. Shouldn't he at least hear boards settling? A loud snore from a neighbor? Water running through the pipes or central air kicking on and off? Or was the top floor so well-insulated—so isolated—that sound didn't carry up here?

Coop scraped his palm over the late-night stubble shading his jaw. What was a single woman doing, living alone in this big empty place where there were no neighbors to run to for help, no one to hear her in the middle of a night like this, even if she screamed?

Hurrying his pace, Coop quickly reached the single, sliding steel door marked "400." He raised his fist and knocked. "Sarah?" He pushed the buzzer, then knocked a little harder, hating how his random observations about the building had spooked him into this wary state. Why the hell wasn't she answering the door? Maybe Seth had been right to be concerned. Despite the apartment's fortresslike design, he wouldn't want one of his own sisters to be so cut off from the rest of the world. He pounded. "Sarah!"

The door slid open beneath his fist.

"Coop? What are you doing here?"

Dropping his hand to his side, he swept his gaze over all five feet and not much more of Sarah Cartwright.

Ah, hell. The summery scents of peaches and mango drifted up to his nose, igniting a decidedly nonbrotherly awareness of the woman standing in the doorway. She wore a modest pair of pajamas, with one of those strappy knit tops, and plaid pants that were rolled up at the ankle.

But it was the damp spots clinging to the tops of her small breasts and the flat of her stomach that made the whole package so unexpectedly sexy. She'd come straight from the shower, looking fresh-scrubbed and fragile and utterly feminine—from the damp, darkened strands of her towel-dried hair to the pink painted nails on her tiny bare feet.

For a couple of heartbeats, Cooper forgot why he was standing at this door in the shadows before dawn. It was always like this for him, and it always took him a second to come up with the right teasing line to remind him that this was his partner's sister he was lusting after.

"Coop?" Sarah brushed past him, looking up and down the empty hallway before tilting those pretty green eyes all the way up to his following gaze. "I thought they'd send a uniformed officer."

That's when the frown between the eyes registered, along with the antsy way she rubbed her palms and tapped her fingers together.

Coop's smile flatlined. "Why do you need a uniformed officer?" That same wariness that had itched beneath the surface of his skin on the way up returned in full force. He wrapped one big hand around both of hers, stilling her twisting fingers. "Sarah?"

She startled with a gasp, as if his touch had interrupted some deep thought process. But instead of pulling away, she turned her hands inside his grasp and held on. "I'm glad you're here. I could use a friendly face right about now."

Damn. Despite the warmth of a shower, her skin was generating nothing but chill.

"C'mon." With a gentle tug, he pulled her back into the apartment, slid the heavy door shut and locked it behind him. He nudged her toward the center of the open living space, then quickly moved past her to check the windows for signs of trouble. Maybe there'd been a break-in. But every window was solid, locked tight. The bedroom area, untouched. The kitchen area was equally clean. The bathroom was a mess of dirty clothes and damp towels, as though she'd stripped and showered and changed more than once.

Ah, hell. A very bad feeling throbbed in the tight clench of his jaw. His nostrils flared as he forced himself to breathe deeply, to check his emotions and silence the bombardment of questions that begged to be asked.

He turned back to Sarah, looking small and vulnerable where she stood in the middle of the room. She stared at a spot on the wooden floor, hugging herself, shivering.

"Sarah?" Coop slowly approached her, demanding that those big green eyes meet his. "Why do you need a cop?"

She didn't disappoint. Smoothing a damp strand of hair off her face, she lifted her gaze. "To answer my 9-1-1 call."

"All right. Back up and start this conversation from the beginning." Any pretense of standing in as big brother vanished with the tears that glistened in the fringe of her lashes. Something had happened. Something very bad. The wary detective in him was already on guard, already alert. But the man in him needed to touch her, needed to make whatever had gone wrong right. He reached out to brush aside the stubborn lock of hair that still stuck to her cheek. "What 9-1-1 call?"

"I…" The instant his finger touched her, a huge sigh rattled through her from tip to toe. Instead of talking, she turned and walked into him, wrapping her arms around his waist. "Hold me."

She aligned herself against him, cheek to chest, breast to stomach, thigh to thigh.

A burst of heat radiated through him in every place they touched. Something tight and controlled inside him began to melt.

Coop hesitated a moment before giving in to the heat and the need and winding his arms tightly around her. He rested his chin on the top of her head and wrapped his body around her, surrounding her in his strength and warmth. Seth was gonna kill him for this. But Sarah snuggled closer, and he couldn't push her away. He heard the sniffles, felt the clutch of her fingers at the back of his waist. Moments later, the warmth of her tears dampened the front of his T-shirt and singed his skin. *He* was gonna kill someone if this innocent woman had been hurt. "Sarah, you never answered—"

"Just hold me." Her lips moved against his sensitized skin, and his body leaped with the need to respond in some elemental way.

He rubbed circles up and down her spine, pressed a kiss to the crown of her head and rested his nose in the fragrant silk of her freshly washed hair.

"I've gotcha."

The cop in him would have to wait.

Chapter Two

Three months later

"What do you mean, we've got nothing on Theodore Wolfe? I thought Wolfe International was history." Seth Cartwright's question fueled an outburst of debates around the KCPD headquarters briefing room.

"Their money-laundering setup here in K.C., yes. And we've put a serious dent in their drug profits by shutting down their Kansas City base. But we've still got some loose ends to tie up," replied Captain John Kincaid in his typically cool, calm and collected tone. The grumbles subsided. He gripped the desktop podium and leaned forward to make sure every detective and uniformed officer in the room understood how serious he was. "Understand this. I intend to nail the big boss and give KCPD the credit for his arrest before they kick me upstairs to the deputy commissioner's office."

Leaning back in his chair at the front table, Cooper Bellamy crossed his long legs at the ankle and sipped his coffee as another round of should-haves and what-ifs and let's-do-its ensued. His own partner, Seth, turned to the long table behind them and questioned Kincaid's second-eldest son, Sawyer, another young detective, to see if he had any insight into his father's plans for the case.

Coop seemed to take it all in with half an ear. His disinterest was deceptive, though. He was as frustrated as his partner to hear how progress had stalled on their investigation into Wolfe International's illegal activities.

Captain Kincaid, the man who'd recruited Coop and Seth from the Fourth precinct to work on his organized-crime task force, raised his hands and quieted the room with little more than a stern fatherly look. Coop sat up straight, remembering that same look from his own father. A gung-ho Marine until the day his job took his life, Clint Bellamy had high expectations from all five of his children, especially his oldest son, Coop. And though he'd managed to inject plenty of laughter into their lives when he'd been home, Clint's rules for living had been drilled in hard and often.

Respect for authority went without saying. And Captain Kincaid had earned it.

Being there for the team—whether that meant backing up his partner or taking care of his mother and younger brothers and sisters—was another tenet in the Bellamy code.

But the rule that had him sitting up and waiting for the captain to explain their next plan of action was that no matter what it required of a man, failure on a mission was not an option.

Coop thumped his partner's shoulder, urging him to ease up on the second-guessing. "Let's hear what the big dog has to say."

The room quieted, and the captain recapped the task force's accomplishments and remaining goals.

Theodore Wolfe's son, Teddy, Jr., had been killed in a shootout with Seth when Teddy had tried to murder the woman who had since become Seth's fiancée. Although one of Teddy's partners appeared to be a legitimate K.C. businessman, their casino had been temporarily closed until the Treasury Department could straighten out the books. And Teddy's right-hand man and Wolfe International enforcer, Shaw McDonough—the man Sarah Cartwright had identified as a cold-blooded killer—had gone AWOL.

McDonough had skipped the country. His plane ticket out of KCI said Bermuda, but authorities had had no luck tracking him down there. They couldn't even confirm that he'd actually gotten off the plane. The bastard could be anywhere on the planet. Spending his money in the Caribbean. Living under an assumed name back in London, still doing his boss's dirty work. Murdering someone else if the price was right.

Coop set down his coffee as the taste went bitter. That fateful night when Sarah had witnessed the murder of Teddy's mistress had changed his life, too. And not for the better. He'd screwed up when he'd gone to check on her. He hadn't been thinking with his brain. He'd misread signals and moved way too fast. At the very least, his timing had sucked. He'd risked his heart and gotten it thrown back in his face for his troubles—and jeopardized his friendship with Seth should the whole truth of those twenty-four hours together with Sarah ever come out.

"So what are we supposed to do, Captain? Sit back on our heels and let Wolfe International peddle its influence somewhere else?" Seth's question was a welcome interruption to Coop's self-damning thoughts.

His gaze strayed to the photograph posted on the screen at the front of the room. Theodore Wolfe, Sr. Black hair, silver temples. He could have been a member of Parliament with that high-class suit and demeanor. But there was a much darker side to the multimillionaire mob boss who ruled a gambling empire that touched four continents.

Wolfe was controller of everything he touched. Rich as Midas and as feared as Hades himself. Not a nice guy.

KCPD may have put a stop to his son's criminal career, but Daddy and his number-one henchman remained untouched.

"No, Cartwright." There was no doubt that the captain had command of the room. "I intend to nail Wolfe on our turf. We've got unfinished business with him here. He's responsible for ordering the death of crime reporter Reuben Page—" the father of Seth's fiancée, Rebecca "—and Danielle Ballard, the intern who was feeding Page information on the bribes Wolfe offered key economic development and zoning committee members."

"So that disk Rebecca and I found at the Riverboat casino proves Wolfe's influence?" Seth asked.

Captain Kincaid nodded. "Absolutely. Plus, Mac Taylor from the forensic lab says he's got a clean bullet from Dawn Kingsley's body that matches the one he took from Reuben Page three years earlier. If we can get him McDonough's gun, we can link him to both murders and send McDonough to death row."

Along with Sarah's eyewitness testimony.

"Captain?" Coop had to pipe up with a smart remark sooner or later, or Seth would suspect that something heavy was weighing on his thoughts, and start asking him questions he didn't want to answer. "You really think Wolfe and McDonough are stupid enough to return to the scene of the crime?"

"Not stupidity. Arrogance. And family honor." Coop had to admire the captain's thorough profiling of their targets. "If one or both of those men don't show up to avenge Teddy's death at the hands of KCPD, I'll be surprised. Even if they think Teddy was an embarrassment to the family and Cartwright did them a favor, they'll be back. Sooner or later. Since Wolfe assumed power of his *company,* he hasn't had a failure."

Cooper grinned. "Until he ran into us badasses here in K.C."

"Something like that." Captain Kincaid chuckled, making it okay for the snickers in the room to erupt into matching, stress-relieving laughter. "On that note, let's start wrapping this thing up. We've got eyes on Wolfe in London, and McDonough's picture is on every airport, shipyard and border crossing watch list. If he tries to re-enter the country, we'll nab him. We'll…"

While the captain began outlining the task force's strategy through the end of the year, Seth leaned over and whispered, "Nice one, buddy. So you think Wolfe is going to come to the States to stick it to us?"

Coop shrugged. "A good businessman is going to

want to show some kind of victory for his investment here in the U.S. Between us and the Treasury Department, we've locked up Wolfe's money. He doesn't want to walk away from here empty-handed. Kincaid's right. One way or another, he'll be back."

Seth sat back with a grin. "You're smarter than you look."

Coop didn't miss a beat. "You're taller than you look."

"Wiseass."

"Pee-wee."

To his credit, Coop's shoulder-high tank of a partner had mellowed in his emotional moods since finding a woman who could go head to head with him in any battle of words and wills. They could give each other grief, and Seth would walk away smiling with a genuine sense of peace he hadn't known for a long time.

Coop hid his pensive smile behind another swallow of his tepid morning coffee, swallowing the guilt that nagged at his conscience right along with it. His friendship with Seth Cartwright went deep, and he wouldn't begrudge the tough guy his well-earned contentment.

Funny how finding a soul mate could reform even the hardest of hearts. Seth and Rebecca Page deserved their happily-ever-after. And come Christmas time, he'd proudly stand up as best man when the two of them got married.

Coop's mind wandered from the captain's spiel about timetables and task force goals.

Serving as best man might be as close as he'd ever get to a wedding himself. Not unless he could find a way to purge Sarah Cartwright from his thoughts the same way she seemed to have erased him from her life so quickly and thoroughly.

It had started as a simple kiss that morning in July. Coop had stood by Sarah while a uniformed officer had taken her statement and gotten contact information. He'd held her hand while the officer had promised to post an APB for both a man named McDonough and the blond girl's body. Sarah had witnessed a murder at the Riverboat Casino. She'd tried to tell Coop something about her father setting her up, something about Teddy Wolfe using her.

And then she'd started crying again before everything made sense. When she'd walked into his arms a second time, Cooper had welcomed her, held her tight. When she'd asked for a kiss, he hadn't been able to resist.

That kiss had seemed to go on and on. Instead of stopping, it had altered, deepened—demanded—and comfort had given way to passion.

It had been quick that first time. Crazy.

She needed him, she'd said. Needed that affirmation of life, of normalcy. She'd needed that soul-deep connection to another human being that making love could provide. And Coop had wanted to help her so badly—had wanted *her* so badly—that he hadn't been able to summon the common sense to refuse her anything she asked.

"I'm sorry." She'd started apologizing before they'd even had all their clothes back on. *"I took advantage of your kindness, your caring. I'm no better than—"*

"Hey, that wasn't completely unexpected between the two of us, was it? Things have been simmering for months. Trust me, kindness had nothing to do with how

much I wanted you." He'd tried to draw her back into her bed, had tried to gentle her nervous discomfort with another kiss.

"No. This was a mistake. I wasn't thinking. I'm sorry."

She'd been out of his arms, out of the room before he could get a straight answer about where he'd gone wrong. Then *he* was out of her apartment, and out of her life before he could really get his head around the idea that Sarah Cartwright had only wanted a warm body to get close to that morning.

She hadn't been looking for a relationship.

And she sure as hell hadn't been looking for him.

"Watch it, buddy." Seth nudged Coop's arm, wrenching him back to the present. He nodded toward Coop's hand on the table.

Lukewarm coffee dribbled over the back of Coop's knuckles, leaking from the paper cup he'd crushed in his fist. Damn. *Way to not let this get to you, Bellamy.* But he managed to cover his thoughts with half a grin. "Oops."

"We'll get these bastards. Don't worry." Seth had misread Coop's frustration, but his reassurance offered an easy excuse.

"I know. We'll get 'em."

While Coop mopped at the mess with a paper napkin, John Kincaid finished his briefing. "I'll contact you individually with your assignments as they come up. In the meantime, return to your normal duties at your home precinct." Coop tossed the cup and napkin into a nearby trash can as the captain dismissed them. "And remember to keep a twenty-four-hour line of contact open. We want to be able to mobilize our team the instant something new breaks on this case."

"Yes, sir," Coop answered, joining the chorus of responses from the task force members as they stood and filed from the room. Wadding up a handful of paper towels from the sink near the exit, he traded gibes and snippets of friendly conversation with his fellow cops as they walked past. Soon it was just him wiping down the table where he'd spilled his coffee, and Seth, waiting at the door for him so they could ride back to the Fourth Precinct building together.

A soft knock at the door echoed in the room's sudden quiet.

"Hey, kiddo."

Coop recognized what Seth's familiar greeting meant. He braced for the figurative punch in the gut, even before he turned around to see his partner swallow up his twin sister in a hug.

"Hey, Seth." Sarah planted a kiss on her brother's cheek as she pulled away.

Coop stood back and watched, remembering, comparing that chaste kiss to the brazen thrust of her tongue in his mouth. *Damn.* Muscles clenched in hidden places, and he was suffused with a sudden heat that made him itchy beneath his skin.

He turned away while the brother and sister, who obviously shared such a deep connection, caught up on the past couple of weeks since they'd last seen each other. He couldn't deny them the joy this impromptu reunion gave them, not when Coop shared the same kind of bond with his own family. But he didn't have to stand there and watch and want, and wonder how he could be jealous of Seth—Sarah's brother. Coop's partner. His best friend.

Feeling like an unwanted fly at a picnic, Cooper concentrated very hard on carrying the coffee-soaked towels to the trash and dumping them. If there was a back door to this tenth-floor meeting room, he'd already be gone.

"Hey, Coop."

Was that a hesitation he heard in Sarah's voice? Or was that just his own reluctance to act like nothing had changed between them when everything felt different— twisted—inside him. Of course, *he'd* made the effort to call her, to stop by her apartment. But her absences and lack of response had made it embarrassingly clear that he was the only one interested in making something happen between them. Or, at the very least, he was the only one interested in making sense of what had felt like a real relationship to him for about twelve hours or so.

So hell, yeah. If she could pretend nothing had happened that morning, then so could he. Coop strolled over to the doorway to join them, grabbing his KCPD ball cap and pasting on a grin along the way. "Hey, Sarah. So what brings you to Cop Land?"

"I was hoping I could take you to lunch."

She was still a pint-sized ball of pretty. Neither time nor distance nor three months of a cold shoulder that could have raised goose bumps diminished that fact. Today she wore a denim jumper over a deep-green turtleneck that brought out the color of her eyes. Her wheat-and-honey-colored ponytail was the only evidence of the tomboy she'd once been, because there was nothing boyish about the slightly crooked, all sexy mouth beneath the peachy tint of her lipstick.

"I'll leave you to it. If you need a ride back to the precinct, Seth, just give me a call." Coop circled around him and tried to slide out the door without touching Sarah. "See ya."

"I meant you, Coop." He paused at the tug on his sleeve. But when he turned to look down at the hand on his arm, Sarah quickly folded her fingers into her palm and tucked her fist back under the jacket she'd draped over her forearms. "My treat."

The upturned eyes pleaded but didn't explain the out-of-the-blue request. What the hell?

"Hey, what about *me?*" Seth protested. "Don't I rate an invitation?"

Sarah turned back to her brother, leaving Coop to quiz the possibilities on his own. "I happen to know that Rebecca is picking you up downstairs at noon. She said she has plans for you today." She cocked her head to one side. "Something about china patterns and silverware?"

Seth groaned and reached over her to clasp Coop by the shoulder. "Save me."

"Hey, don't look at me. You're the one who proposed." It was easier to joke than to let anything get too serious with Sarah standing between them. "I see you as sort of a 'pewter goblet' kind of guy myself."

"I *am* wearing a gun, remember?"

"Cut it out, you two," Sarah chided them both. "Look, if it makes you feel any better, Rebecca did say something about being able to get the job done in twenty minutes and then having the rest of her lunch break to do whatever it is you two do when you have...free time together?" The wink-wink teasing in her voice was obvious.

And Seth was eating it up. "Hmm. I think pickin' out dishes just got a little more interesting."

"You wish, Cartwright." Coop had rarely seen a smile on his partner's face during the eight long months he'd worked undercover at the casino and gotten cozy with the mob. He wasn't about to douse Seth's well-deserved happiness by bringing up anything like the fact he'd slept with his sister and then hadn't spoken to her for twelve weeks. Even if the latter hadn't been his choice.

Seth was already anxious to leave. "So what are you two going to do? If you're ganging up as best man and maid of honor to pull some kind of prank at the reception or the bachelor party, you can just forget it." He pointed a stern finger at Sarah. "I know you're a good girl, but you...?"

Coop threw his hands up in mock surrender at the accusatory finger now pointed his way. "I'm a good girl, too."

"Yeah, right." Seth's laugh demanded that Coop and Sarah join in, too. "You guys have fun." He kissed his sister's cheek, then poked that finger against Coop's chest. "Not too much fun, though. You mind your manners."

Sarah nudged her brother down the hallway. "I'll make sure he does. Now go. Don't keep Rebecca waiting."

Seth spared them a glance over his shoulder. "I guess I won't be needing to bum that ride back to the Fourth. I'll have Bec drop me off after we...lunch."

"Braggart."

With a laugh, Seth strutted off toward the elevators.

The hallway outside the briefing room was awkwardly quiet, now that Coop was alone with Sarah.

"Wow." Sarah hugged her jacket to her waist and watched her brother all the way until his parting salute from behind the closing elevator doors. "I haven't seen Seth this happy in months. He's like the young guy he used to be before…" Her voice trailed away as though she was surprised to discover just how distasteful the end of that sentence was going to be. She leveled her shoulders and turned back to Coop. "Who'd have thought his arch-nemesis Rebecca Page would turn out to be so good for him?"

"Yeah. Who'd've thunk?" Coop agreed. Sarah's gaze danced to the left. He studied the corduroy collar on her jacket. Yeah, this was awkward. "Don't you have school today?" he asked, needing to hear something besides strained silence.

Green eyes met his. "I took the morning off. I had a doctor's appointment."

A flare of genuine concern made him lean in half a step. He understood bad news from the doctor better than most. "Are you sick? Hurt?"

She inhaled and slowly released a deep breath that did nothing to ease his worry. "Is there someplace private we can talk?" she asked.

"This is KCPD headquarters. Someone's always watchin' around here."

His lame attempt at humor earned nothing more than a blink. "I'm serious, Coop."

Yeah, *that* was reassuring.

So, had she finally gotten around to analyzing what

had happened between them? Maybe this was the clean break he'd been hoping for, yet dreading at the same time. And if there was truly some bad news...

Cooper looked beyond her to the noise and bustle of administrative support staff working at their desks in the floor's main room. With pairs and groups of blue suits and detectives still standing around and discussing the task force meeting and other business, he and Sarah weren't going to find any privacy out there. He looked back toward the row of reinforced glass windows that formed the near wall of the briefing room. Even if they went inside and closed the door, anyone could look through the windows and see them together. And too much time spent alone with Sarah—in deep conversation or a possible argument—would surely get back to Seth. And Coop didn't want to answer to that one.

The sun was shining outside. The air was crisp but not cold. Coop angled his head toward the exit. "Let's go for a walk."

Turning, Sarah led the way to the elevator. Coop pulled his hat over his bare head and, hanging back far enough so that he couldn't reach out and touch her, followed behind.

SARAH WAS AFRAID THE QUEASY sensation in her stomach had nothing to do with the elevator ride or the secret she carried inside her.

Instead, she worried it had a lot to do with the tall, lanky detective leaning against the railing on the far side of the elevator. There was a guarded awareness to his deceptively relaxed stance. A curious introspection to the hooded blue eyes that watched the buttons light up with each floor they passed. Cooper Bellamy's unnatural silence on the ride down to the main floor was all the proof she needed that she had done him a terrible wrong.

She'd traded a friend for a lover that morning when she'd been so afraid, so confused, so desperate to cling to his sheltering strength. And now she had neither. She'd felt more wanted, more necessary to someone in that first long kiss she'd shared with Cooper Bellamy than she'd felt in the weeks or months she'd spent dating anyone else. But the discovery couldn't have come at a worse time.

She'd been fooled once by Teddy Wolfe. Fooled more times than she could count by her own father. How could she believe anything a man told her? How could she believe in anything she felt?

Humiliation was a hard thing to admit to, and losing that last shred of trust in her father had been a painful lesson to learn. Sarah's shameful silence these past weeks had been about curling up in a hole and licking her wounds. It was easier to be alone—to work and sleep and nothing more—than it was to doubt other trusts she had given, to fear the consequences of other choices she had made. At least alone, she could inflict no more damage on her own fragile sense of self, or on anyone else she dared to care about.

But then the naps had become more frequent, had lasted longer. She had caught a feverless flu bug that hit about the same time every morning if she didn't snack between breakfast and lunch. A blue dot on a little plastic stick had confirmed what she'd already suspected. The report from her Ob/Gyn this morning had made the dreaded news official.

Sarah couldn't hide anymore.

A woman was dead. Her murderer had skipped the country. Sarah's deposition was on record, but without a killer to put on trial, her testimony was useless. Teddy Wolfe was dead, by her brother's hand, so there was no way to confront him for what he had done, no satisfaction to be gained by exposing him for the player he was. And even if she hadn't severed every connection with her pimp of a father, there was no helping him with his addiction.

Sarah was helpless. Useless. She could do nothing to make things right.

But she could be honest.

As she stole a glance at the man reflected in the elevator's polished steel doors, she knew she owed Cooper Bellamy that much.

They'd left the elevator and crossed through the security checkpoint on the first floor before Coop said his next word.

"Here." After shrugging into his own Army-issue camo-print jacket, he pulled her canvas barn coat from her twisting arms and held it so she could switch her purse from hand to hand and slide her arms into the sleeves.

"Thanks."

He pushed open the door that led to the building's granite steps down to the sidewalk and street. When a trio of uniformed police officers met them coming up the steps, Coop touched his hand to the small of her back and guided her to the side, out of their path.

His gentlemanly considerations surprised her. The speed with which he did the job and broke contact with her did not. Feeling the chill of his aversion to her as much as the bite of the autumn breeze on her cheeks, Sarah buttoned her jacket and thrust her hands into its deep pockets.

The touch of his fingers at her elbow burned through canvas and cotton, but only long enough to dodge traffic as they crossed the street and headed north toward a clearing dotted with trees and benches and modern sculptures. "The park looks pretty empty. We can walk through it up to the courthouse and back."

"That'd be fine." The city block that had been cleared of condemned buildings and reclaimed to offer a spot of beauty in the midst of downtown renovations should have been a balm to her frazzled nerves and traitorous stomach. The oaks and maples were studded with red and orange leaves, while the shrubs surrounding each seating area had turned a rich yellow. But even though a couple shared a bench and a picnic lunch and a pair of women power-walked over its concrete paths, Sarah couldn't share an appreciation for the safety and beauty of the place. She fisted her hands around the strap of her purse and debated how she was going to start this conversation. None of the words she'd been rehearsing seemed adequate enough.

They were halfway to the courthouse when Coop broke the silence for her. "So, are we just gonna walk and pretend we've got nothing to say to each other, or is there a point to this exercise?"

Sarah counted the steps off in her head. One. Two. Three. "I'm pregnant."

"What?"

Oh, God. She'd skipped every preamble. Every explanation. Every apology. Was the blood draining from her head? Or was the sidewalk suddenly spinning for some other, more logical reason? "I'm going to have a baby."

"I know what the word means. Do you want me to say congratulations?" He stopped her with a hand on her arm and the world quickly righted itself. But his grip was as tight as the clip of his words. "Or are you lookin' for backup before you tell your old-fashioned brother that you're having a baby without benefit of a husband first?"

"Don't joke, Coop." He pulled away and she took that as a cue to keep walking. "I'm three months along. That makes you the father."

She took four more steps before she realized he'd stopped. When she turned to face him, she saw cold-eyed suspicion filling the laugh lines on his face. "Impossible."

Sarah curled her arms around herself, around the innocent beginnings of life growing inside her. She'd never seen that kind of hardness in Coop's expression before. "You and I didn't use protection that morning. And I wasn't on the pill because I'm not...I wasn't... sexually active."

"It isn't mine."

"Why are you...?" Sarah checked her temper. He had every right to be angry, though she hadn't expected this flat-out denial. "Look, I'm not telling you this because I expect something from you. I'm not looking for a wedding ring or child support or anything."

"Hell. Those things I *can* give you." He turned and

headed back toward headquarters, his long legs quickly putting distance between them.

Sarah hurried to catch up. "You've always been a good friend and I wanted to be up-front about it. Before my belly starts to show and people start asking questions. I didn't want you to think I was hiding it from you."

He whirled around and Sarah backpedaled to keep from running into him. "You slept with someone else." His statement of fact sounded like an accusation. "Or was *I* the fling? Old Coop wasn't good enough? Being together didn't mean a damn thing to you, did it?"

Old? Try virile. Wonderful. Loving. Sarah tilted her head back to absorb every bit of hurt and accusation he hurled from those dark blue eyes. She tried to bring back the familiar kindness with the truth. "It meant everything. I needed you. I needed… But it was too soon. I wasn't ready for emotions to kick in. I couldn't handle anything serious. I may never be able to give you…to give anyone…"

Oh, God. Sarah's strength faltered. Coop's face swam out of focus and her stomach churned. She'd missed her morning snack, lunch was late, the growing baby made such demands on her body. Guilt made such demands on her soul.

She *had* slept with one other man. But they'd used a condom.

Squeezing her lips shut against the roiling protest in her stomach, Sarah opened her purse and fished for the bag of snacks she carried inside. She found the bag but couldn't see the opening, couldn't find the zipper, couldn't get it open. "Damn it."

She swayed. She was falling. She was going to be lying on the grass, losing her breakfast—and Cooper still wouldn't understand the obvious truth. The hopeful truth.

"Sarah?" Strong hands grabbed her by the elbows and took her weight. Her cheek hit soft flannel, and a harder warmth underneath. "C'mon."

Then she was twisting, floating. Sitting on a solid bench with two hands at her waist to steady her, and a firm shoulder in front of her to brace herself against. The spinning in her stomach calmed to a manageable level, and she blinked Cooper's face into focus. He knelt in front of her, his angular features softened with cautious concern. Sarah pulled her hand from his shoulder and traced the line of his jaw.

"You have a good heart. You'd make a wonderful father." But the honest observation turned his concern into a scowl. Feeling an imagined frostbite in her fingertips, Sarah quickly retreated and pulled the bag of fruit and pretzels from her purse. "I'm sorry. I'm not doing this on purpose. I need to eat."

"You should have said something. Here." He took the bag from her fumbling grasp. His fingers worked more surely than hers to open it and pull out a bag of pretzels and an apple. "Which do you want?"

He opened the pretzels she reached for and zipped the apple back into the bag. The salty snack was tasteless on her tongue and dry going down her throat. But the effect on her stomach was almost instantaneous relief.

Coop waited for her to eat a palmful before speaking again. The bite of sarcasm had left his voice, but an unfamiliar hardness shaded his eyes and aged his expression. "Look, I knew you were upset about sleeping with me. But I thought it was because you preferred to have me in your life as a brother—or you were worried about it messing with Seth's and my working relationship. I had no idea you regretted it because you were already sleeping with someone else."

"Stop saying that. I wasn't seeing anyone. I mean, you weren't…" Sarah stopped chewing and swallowed. *No, no, no, no, no.* She and Teddy had done it once. Thankfully, she'd made him use a condom. It had been embarrassingly quick. Awful. A terrible mistake. But accidents happened. She and Coop had thrown caution to the wind. It had been beautiful. Natural. Redeeming. Perfect. She curled her arm around her stomach and looked deep into those blue eyes, willing him to understand. This *had* to be Coop's baby. "We spent all morning in bed, making—"

"I can't father a child."

Sarah shook her head, desperate to make sense of Cooper's hurtful words. Tears stung her eyes, but she blamed the hormones and swiped them away before they could fall. "It *has* to be you."

"I didn't use protection because we didn't need to." Coop pushed to his feet and sat beside her with a resigned sigh. He pulled off his cap and rubbed his handsome, shiny head. Not a style choice. A consequence. "You know I had cancer, right?"

She nodded. "Sure. Seth talked about it. He said you were in college at the time—before he knew you. But he said you were okay. I mean, look at you. You're a strong, strapping…" Suddenly stricken with real compassion,

Sarah reached out and curled her fingers around his forearm. "Oh, my God. You're not sick again, are you?"

He shrugged off her touch as if it repulsed him. "No. My cancer's history. I take care of myself. I go in for regular follow-ups. I've been cancer-free for five years now. With surgery and radiation, I beat the damn monster. But not without some collateral damage."

Sarah tilted her gaze to the top of his head. "So you can't grow hair."

"And I can't make babies."

Coop was raw inside. He never talked about this. But Sarah's news hurt so damn much. It was like the army officers at the front door. The no-nonsense doctor in the tiny exam room.

Sarah wasn't his—never had been. Still, he felt betrayed.

In a perfect world, he'd be the only man in her life. But there was nothing perfect about his dad being killed in action, then finding out the same month he had a tiny tumor growing in his prostate gland.

He'd *had* to beat the cancer. Not for his sake, but for his mother's. And for Katharine, James, Grace and Clint, Jr. His family needed him to step up and be the man of the house. He had to be the strength, the financing, the discipline, the love and support in his father's place. Sure, there were government benefits. Every Bellamy worked, from part-time jobs to paper routes. His dad's older brother, Walt, now a retired professor from the University of Missouri, had sent money and offered help however he could.

But *he* had to be the man. He had to be there for the

day-to-day stuff. Sacrifices had to be made. And Coop, a young man who hadn't even reached the prime of his life yet, had done it willingly.

The urologist had warned him there'd be a change in his sex life. Oh, the plumbing all worked now, worked just fine. But there was something like a ninety-nine-percent chance he could *never* make the miracle of life happen. All his little Coopers had been sacrificed so that he could live.

To take care of his family.

To become a cop.

To love and lose out big-time.

Sarah needed to hear the truth. *He* needed to hear the reason why he'd kept his distance from a woman who seemed so crazy-right for him that, even now, he wanted to wrap her up in his arms and kiss some color back into her cheeks. But he wouldn't be that much of a fool. He needed to remind himself why he should have walked away that morning instead of giving in to what he thought they'd both wanted. "I'm sterile."

"Sterile?" she echoed. If possible, her skin grew even more pale.

"You may be pregnant…" Maybe some bastard had broken her heart. Maybe the father didn't mean any more to her than Coop did. But the sympathy she wanted, the acceptance she'd expected, wouldn't come. "But that baby isn't mine."

Chapter Three

He brushed aside the first leaves to fall and splayed his fingers over the cold red marble that marked Danielle Ballard's grave.

Washington Cemetery was a beautiful, tranquil place—except for that nosy groundskeeper who'd asked too many curious questions about his visit so late in the day. It didn't matter that it was closing time and that that peon had been ready to shut and lock the gates. He'd come a long way to see Dani. To see the woman he loved.

No one would keep him from her.

He picked at the blood that was drying beneath his manicured nails and stood. He could get used to living in Kansas City. The tree-studded hills away from the heart of downtown reminded him of the Lake District back in England. The rustle of wind through the autumn leaves reminded him of his boyhood in Keswick. Of course, he'd become a Londoner by the necessity of his job description—and there were perks to that historic and sophisticated city, which he'd miss.

There was history here, too, albeit the Wild West-cowboy kind. The city had theater and music and art. And though Kansas City had nothing to rival any Manchester United powerhouse, there was even a decent football— or soccer, as they called it in the States—team here.

He could buy box seats at the games, become a patron of one of the museums. He could even put up a stake and reopen the damned casino if Mr. Wolfe thought it could still be a useful front. He would definitely reopen the drug pipeline that had shown such potential for growth had it been managed properly. Some of the players were still in place. Other slots could easily be filled. With his strong hand, the distribution network could be reestablished, deadlines and quotas enforced, and he'd be raking in money in a way that Teddy Wolfe never had.

He'd done the groundwork to create Wolfe International's presence in the Midwest—on both the legitimate and more profitable business fronts. He'd done the jobs Teddy hadn't had the stomach to deal with. And despite Teddy's crash-and-burn over one woman too many and a clever deception by KCPD, the law had never touched *him.* He was smarter. Stronger. More loyal to Theodore Wolfe than his own son, Teddy, had ever been.

He deserved the opportunity to run the Wolfe empire.

"Shaw? Are you listening to me?"

He bristled at the impatient demand in his employer's slickly accented voice. One day, Theodore Wolfe, Sr., would be down on his knees, begging *him* for favors.

"Don't call me Shaw, sir." The old governor might slip, without even realizing it, and give him away.

· "Not to worry. This call can't be traced. And I simply can't get my head around your new name."

"Then don't use any name."

But Theodore Wolfe, builder and boss of the Wolfe International empire, didn't take criticism well. "I paid for your face and name. I'll call you anything I damn well like."

The man once known as Shaw McDonough bit his tongue. "Of course, Mr. Wolfe. I was merely thinking of the assignment you gave me. Avenging your son's death?"

"His murder," Wolfe corrected. Good. Let the old man be the one having the emotional reaction. He'd learned the hard way that rational thinking and careful planning for every contingency were the only ways to guarantee survival in this business. "Have you tracked down Seth Cartwright?"

He laughed. The old man didn't even know he was already in Kansas City. "I haven't failed you yet. Don't worry, I've set things in motion to get Cartwright's attention."

"I want the entire family to pay. He needs to hurt the same way I do."

It was because of Seth Cartwright, and others like him at KCPD, that he had been brought to this place. He pulled a pink, long-stemmed rose from the bouquet at his feet and kissed the bud. "We've all suffered a tremendous loss here, sir. Trust me, they'll pay."

"Are you certain you want to do this? I have other men I can call."

"Oh, I want to do this." A reporter named Reuben Page and his story about the Wolfe family had forced him into this position. Danielle had worked for the city, coordinating communications between the economic development committee and the gaming commission.

She'd fed Page information on bribes Teddy Wolfe had paid council members. He'd had no qualms about silencing Page and his story. Teddy had even been on hand, talking tough like he was the one pulling the trigger. But interest from KCPD and men like Seth Cartwright had forced him to take his job one step further. His sworn loyalty to Theodore Wolfe had left him no choice but to silence the woman he loved. It was only right that he be repaid for his loss. "I'll take down the Cartwrights for you and put an end to the task force's investigation."

What happened after that would remain his own little secret.

"Call if you need anything." Theodore Wolfe was dismissing him. "I have men and money in place, ready to assist you."

"You got me back into the country with a new identity." He combed his fingers through the thick wave of dark hair he'd been growing out for months. Danielle would have liked it. She'd always said his short cut was too severe. But covering the strands of gray and growing it out wasn't the only obvious change in his appearance. "That's enough for now. If I need anything else, I'll let you know."

"They killed my boy, Shaw. Teddy may have been a disappointment, but he was my flesh and blood. That can't go unpunished."

"It won't. You'll keep to our agreement?"

"You're the closest thing I have to a son now. Do what I ask, and everything I own in the States is yours."

Shaw McDonough disconnected the overseas call.

He pressed the phone against his temple and flipped it shut. Then he placed the pink rosebud over Danielle's name and straightened.

The hour was late, but there was something pleasant, freeing, about the cooling night air. Tomorrow would be soon enough to begin his work. He'd spend a little more time with Danielle. Maybe he'd eat one of those famous Kansas City steaks tonight. Then he'd sleep. God, how he needed to sleep.

It felt good to be back in Kansas City. Good to be back where there was so much to do. Good to be back with Danielle.

"I love you, Dani."

A few minutes later he walked down the hill to the rented car he'd parked there.

It would be good to finally get what was rightfully his.

SARAH WATCHED HER fourth graders run from the monkey bars to the climbing pit, argue over whose turn it was in an impromptu game of kickball and huddle together at the edge of the playground to discuss the plans and secrets that nine- and ten-year-olds loved to talk about. Normally, one of the aides brought her students out for afternoon recess while she graded papers or prepped the next lesson, but today she needed the fresh air.

She needed something to stir her from the disturbing thoughts that had given her a fitful sleep last night and had plagued her all day long.

"I'm sterile."

How could that be possible? Cooper Bellamy was a

kid at heart, with a wise man's soul. He'd lived through the worst the world had to offer and had come out a stronger man for it—strong enough to keep his sense of humor and not turn bitter. He'd make a wonderful father, combining just the right amount of softie and strength.

But he couldn't be a father. He could never pass on those tall, blue-eyed genes.

That meant…

Sarah didn't even want to think of the alternative. She caught a strand of hair the breeze kept trying to free and tucked it back behind her ear. Concentrating on the small, mindless task offered a brief respite from the inevitable truth she had to face.

Her brief affair with Teddy Wolfe had left her ego in shreds, her faith in men in shambles. She'd been leading with her heart all her life—loving, forgiving, trusting. What an idiot she'd been, thinking the father she'd protected for so long would protect her in return, thinking the man she desired would desire her in the same way.

Now she couldn't even trust her own judgment. The instincts she'd always believed in had led her astray. She'd gotten herself pregnant by a mobster who was now dead. A man surrounded by deception and murder. . A man she couldn't form any cherished memories over because he'd used her merely as a means to an end. He must have loved that other woman—Dawn—whom she'd seen shot and killed and bundled away—if he was even capable of loving. Teddy wasn't the man she'd thought he was.

Neither was her father.

But Coop…

Sarah turned her face into the breeze to keep the hair off her face. She warned one of her boys down from the top of the monkey bars, checked the time and quickly scanned the rest of the play area to make sure all were safe and accounted for in the last five minutes of play time. But she couldn't shake the images of heat and hardness against her skin. Of tender, husky praises against her ear. Of seductive, demanding lips against her own.

Lying in Cooper Bellamy's arms had been healing and foolish and wonderful. She was ashamed to think that she'd taken advantage of his long-time friendship. She'd been so frightened, so vulnerable. She'd looked to him for acceptance and strength, and he'd been too kind to turn her away.

Coop was caring and funny. Strong. And so intuitively perceptive. He'd known what she needed. Her brother said the same thing about his police work. That he just seemed to know when he needed to show up.

He'd shown up and more. He'd made her feel whole. Clean. He'd made her feel it was safe to trust him.

No wonder he'd acted so betrayed yesterday. He'd been there for her when she'd needed him most. And she'd repaid him by secluding herself without an explanation and getting pregnant by another man.

Cooper Bellamy deserved better.

The thought of carrying Teddy Wolfe's child while a good man like Coop was cheated of fatherhood made her sick to her fragile stomach.

So how was she going to make this right? Short of turning back time and being wiser the second time around, how could she fix this?

"I'm not blaming you, sweetie." She instinctively folded her arm across her waist and let her hand slide down a fraction to caress her belly. As the shock had worn off and she distanced herself from that awful night, she was beginning to fall in love with the child. Being a single mother wouldn't be easy, but it was one challenge she refused to fail. Maybe motherhood was one relationship she could get right. After all, she had a stellar role model in Shauna Cartwright-Masterson.

Oh, damn. Sarah pinched the bridge of her nose and blinked away the tears that suddenly filled her eyes. Her mom was going to make a fabulously cool grandmother. Commissioner of Police. Pretty nifty title for a grandma. Plus, she could cook and bake like nobody's business when she had the time, so she was a winner whether this baby decided to be an overachiever or a homebody or both. *Stupid hormones.* Sarah snuck her fingers up to wipe away the tear that had spilled over.

Maybe she had more to live up to as a single mom than she'd considered. What if she made more stupid choices? What if her baby paid the price for her mistakes?

"Not gonna happen." Sarah rubbed a soothing circle over her stomach, reassuring herself as much as the baby. "None of this is your fault. I'll do better by you. I promise."

The first step would be telling someone besides Coop that she was pregnant. The cool October air had helped her delay the announcement by giving her an excuse to wear layers and loose sweaters that masked her changing shape. Her waist was already thickening and her small breasts seemed to be firmer, if not actually bigger. Though there was no bump to show on her belly yet, she hoped there would be fewer questions later if she started wearing baggy clothes now.

Eventually she'd have to have an explanation for her students. And when the baby arrived in April, she'd have to have arrangements in place with the administration regarding her maternity leave. One of the family dinners she went to with her mom and stepfather, and Seth and his fiancée, Rebecca, would be a perfect opportunity to share the news with the family.

Unless Coop had already leaked her predicament to her brother. *Oh, damn.* Her pulse beat a little faster. Seth would go ballistic. Sure, his temper would be based on concern, but how was she going to explain that the man he'd killed had fathered her baby?

"Miss Cartwright?"

Sarah jumped in her boots as a curly-haired boy tapped her on the arm. Wrenching herself back to the present, back to the playground, she pressed a hand over her racing heart and looked into the dark, apologetic eyes of Angelo Logan. "I'm sorry, Angelo. I was daydreaming."

Content with her excuse, he shrugged and handed her a folded-up note. "The man on the playground said I should give you this."

Alarm bells went off in her head. "What man?"

"I don't know. He was over there." Angelo pointed to the kickball diamond's backstop fence, but Sarah saw no one but the fourth-graders in her class. "Well, he was there. He came up to the fence."

Sarah was already counting heads and hurrying

across the blacktop toward the ball diamond. "What did the man look like?"

Angelo tagged along at her heels. "Somebody's dad."

"Tall? Short? Black? White?"

"He was a white guy." Some of Angelo's buddies had joined them to help with his description. "Well, maybe more Latino. He had black hair, but his skin wasn't dark."

"He had an accent," one boy added. "Maybe he's from India."

"I think he was from Jamaica."

"He wasn't from Jamaica." Angelo was certain of that.

"He was taller than you," another tried to help.

Sarah shook her head. "Everybody's taller than me."

When she reached the fence, she shoved the note into the pocket of her slacks and looked up and down the street, more intent on spotting the stranger who'd ventured onto school grounds than in finding out what he had to say. Cars lined the curb in front of the houses across the street. Was he in one of them? No one was driving away. An elderly couple walking their dog crossed the street, but they both had white hair. A man in sweats jogged around the corner, never once breaking stride nor looking back toward the school.

"Do you see him?" Sarah asked.

The boys looked. "Uh-uh."

"And none of you knew him?"

"No."

Creepy. Dangerous. A little too weird for her.

She needed to protect these kids.

Sarah blew the whistle that hung around her neck.

She pointed to the school's playground doors. "Everybody line up! First one there gets to hand out papers when we get back inside."

An Olympic sprint ensued as students ran and yelled from every direction. Sarah hurried after, counting them off as they formed a line across the blacktop. One, two...twenty-five, twenty-six, twenty-seven.

Thank goodness.

She hugged an arm around Tammy Carlisle's shoulders at the end of the line. All safe and accounted for. "Good job, guys. I see gummy fruits in your future." She summoned a smile for the answering cheers and signaled the boy closest to the door. "You're the man, Derek. Lead us in. Remember to be quiet in the hallway."

Sarah glanced over her shoulder, looking for any signs of movement on the playground or in the surrounding area. But everything was curiously vacant for two-fifteen in the afternoon. That was a good thing, right?

So why couldn't she shake the feeling that someone was watching her or one of the children even now?

Sarah had the students eat their snacks while her aide read the next chapter in *The Twenty-One Balloons* to them before leaving to report the incident to the office. She shut the door behind her and pulled the note from her pocket.

"Oh, my God."

Her principal wasn't the only person she needed to notify.

I'm coming for you.
I'm coming for everyone you love.
But you won't see me until it's too late.

"I GOT ONE, TOO."

Sarah pulled her fingertip from her lips as the dab of sugary frosting on her tongue turned bitter at the calm announcement. She looked across the kitchen table to her future sister-in-law, Rebecca Page. "What did your note say?"

Rebecca shot a pointed glance at Seth as he set his coffee mug down with a thunk beside her. "Same exact words your note contained. Typed out. Not signed. It was in an unsealed envelope in my inbox at the paper."

Seth reached over to brush a dark corkscrew of hair off Rebecca's cheek and smooth it down her back. "And when were you going to tell me this?"

Rebecca smiled. She had her fiancé pegged. "Maybe when I thought you wouldn't overreact the way you're about to right now."

"You know how dangerous Wolfe and his men can be. We can tie at least three murders to his people."

"I haven't forgotten for one minute. But there's no proof the threat came from Wolfe. My father's death isn't the only crime I've written about."

Seth spared Sarah a glance. "Can you name another organized-crime boss who also has a connection to my sister?"

"True." Rebecca's sympathetic gaze blinked, and she turned to Seth. "And there's no sign of Shaw McDonough anywhere?"

Seth squeezed Rebecca's hand, and her strength quickly returned. "As far as we know, he's dropped off the face of the planet."

"But no sign of him is a good thing, isn't it?" She

turned her gaze to Seth and his mother, Shauna, and stepfather, Eli Masterson. But as a cop and former-cop-turned-investigator for the D.A.'s office, they shared Seth's concern.

Sarah tried to help—to alleviate Rebecca's as well as her own fears. "You said he left the country. If KCPD can't find him, that means he's not around to be a threat, right?"

Eli braced his elbows on the table and leaned forward. "The D.A. is prepared to move forward with charges against McDonough if he shows his face again. We'd love to have his gun, knife and explosive devices to create forensic evidence to back up Sarah's testimony. Otherwise, the case would rely almost exclusively on her word. And Rebecca's and Seth's. If McDonough's back in town, that puts this whole family in danger."

So much for reassurance. Sarah's stomach shifted in protest, and she absently rubbed at her tender belly. "So what do we do?"

Shauna answered. "All we can do right now is be extra vigilant. If we focus all our energy on Shaw McDonough, we might overlook a threat from a different direction. From what I've read in John Kincaid's task force reports, Theodore Wolfe has the money to hire anyone he wants. There may be someone new in town who's enforcing his will."

Rebecca's eyes were still on Seth. "Let me guess, you're going to tell me I shouldn't go back to work, you want the names and details of all the stories I'm currently putting together for the *Journal,* and I should stay locked up behind the doors of our apartment." Her cheeks dotted with color. "I mean your—*my* apartment, of course." She swung around to glance at Shauna at the head of the table. "I'm just staying at Seth's until…with our schedules we're not there together a lot."

Sarah snuck the last bite of her cinnamon roll to Sadie, the golden Lab dog lying at her feet beneath the table, hiding a guilty gratitude that the focus of the dinner conversation had shifted away from her and the playground note she'd turned over to KCPD after school. Her heart went out to Rebecca. She couldn't blame her for not wanting to go back to her own apartment where Teddy had been killed. Even after cleaning up the blood and replacing carpets and paint, it would be impossible to forget that her personal haven had been a crime scene. Besides, strong personalities aside, Rebecca and Seth were so clearly in love with each other that it was hard to picture them apart now that they'd found each other.

Sarah's mother offered a smile without commenting on her son and Rebecca's living arrangements. "Did you turn the note over to KCPD?"

Yes, she'd done everything by the book.

"Of course, if the envelope was unsealed, then the lab probably won't be able to get any DNA off it," Shauna went on. They'd already determined that the only fingerprints they'd be able to get off Sarah's note would belong to her and all the children who'd handled it, especially since the one thing her students *could* agree on was that the man who'd given it to them had been wearing gloves. "I'll be sure to notify John about the threats. There's a possibility they may not have anything to do with the Wolfe International investigation, but it's worth a notation in his files."

Seth was less interested in speculation on the case he'd broken open than in discussing something privately with Rebecca. "Could we talk outside for a minute?"

"Ah, it's time for the 'you take too many risks' speech." Rebecca folded her napkin and set it on the table, rising as Seth held her chair. "It was a delicious meal as usual, Mrs. Cartwright-Masterson. Thanks for having me over."

Sarah's mother squeezed Rebecca's hand. "That's a mouthful, isn't it? When are you going to start calling me Shauna?"

"I'll work on that…Shauna."

"See you later, Mom." Seth and Shauna traded hugs and kisses. He kissed the top of Sarah's head. "Kiddo. Be good. Be safe."

"You, too." She and Rebecca exchanged a hug. "Bye."

"Good night, Seth. Rebecca." Eli unfolded his long body from his chair at the opposite end of the table to shake hands with Seth.

"Keep an eye on Mom."

"You know I always do."

"Yeah. Take care." Though his initial opinion of the man their mother had fallen in love with had been somewhere between resentment and outright hostility, Seth had since developed a genuine respect for the man. It probably had something to do with his saving their mother's life, sticking by her when others at KCPD had labeled her a traitor and—loving her like crazy. "I'll talk to you tomorrow. About…things."

"Absolutely."

After Seth and Rebecca had left, Eli turned his dark eyes on the older woman, who was suddenly preoccupied with pouring herself a second cup of decaf coffee. "Shauna?"

"I know that look, Eli."

He propped his hands at his waist, refusing to be put off by her casual attitude. "Did *you* get a note?"

"Mom?" Sarah's fear escalated another notch.

"Same words, same untraceable delivery."

Eli circled the table and rested his hands on Shauna's shoulders. "Are we going to have another incident like we did last fall, when you didn't tell anyone you were in danger?"

"How can I be in danger with you watching over me?" Shauna covered his hands with her own and looked up at him with loving eyes. "I turned the note over to John Kincaid. If these threats are related to his investigation, he'll find out. But between you, me and Seth and Rebecca's reporting career, we've worked hundreds of criminal cases. A lot of people could carry a grudge against our family."

"Yeah, well I'm not going to let them hurt this family. Understood?"

"Understood. Neither will I." After some kind of secret signal, Eli leaned down and kissed her.

The kiss was short enough to be polite with company at the table, but intimate enough that Sarah bent down to pet the dog and pretended she wasn't feeling any pangs of loneliness. She was truly happy that her mother had finally found a good man to love, happy for Seth and Rebecca. Maybe that was why she'd been so blinded by Teddy Wolfe's interest in her. She'd just wanted to find a little bit of that happiness, too. She couldn't help feeling a trace of envy when her own prospects for a happily-ever-after seemed so far out of reach.

Now, it looked as though her future would include only her and the baby.

And some crazy who claimed he was coming for her. Coming for all of them. *Damn.*

Sarah excused herself to the restroom to splash some cool water on her face and to give her mom and Eli some privacy.

When she returned to the kitchen to help with the dishes, her mom had already cleared the table, and Eli was out walking Sadie. Sarah grabbed a towel and picked up a baking dish to dry it. For several minutes, the two women worked in companionable silence.

After Shauna put the last pan in the draining rack, she started the dishwasher and wiped down the counters. "Do you think Rebecca is ever going to relax around me?"

"You *are* the future mother-in-law," Sarah pointed out with a smile. "I think she recognizes another strong woman and is worried about impressing you."

"She shouldn't be. She brought my son back to the land of the living. So I love her already."

Sarah nodded. Rebecca had put up a tough facade when first meeting her, but, like Seth, she'd seen behind the protective armor. Now Sarah had a new friend, and her brother was a happy man. "She'll come around soon enough."

"I hope so." Shauna hung up the dishcloth and pulled the towel from Sarah's hands to dry her own. "But enough about Seth and Rebecca. Are you going to tell me what's bothering you?"

Zing. She'd been blindsided. Must be the fatigue, or she would have anticipated the motherly concern switching targets. "I'm fine."

"Come on." Her mother took her by the hand and led her to the kitchen table, where she urged her to sit and share, just as they had so many times in the past. "I raised you, young lady. Your brother is the moody one. You're the one with the hugs and smiles and positive thinking."

Sarah resisted the urge to pull her hands down to her stomach and shield the secret she wasn't quite ready to share. "I'm just tired. I'm probably fighting a bug of some kind. There have been plenty of coughs and sniffles at school the past couple of weeks."

Shauna's green eyes narrowed, seeing things only a mother could see. "I understand how receiving a threat like that can shake you. And knowing you, you're probably more worried about your students' safety than your own. But this is something else."

"No." But her smile rang false.

"Is it Dawn Kingsley's murder? You did speak to the trauma counselor I recommended, didn't you?"

"Yes," she reassured her. "The nightmares aren't as much of a problem as they used to be."

But her mother wasn't convinced. "I want to say it's the flu that has you looking so pale and is playing games with your appetite. But I don't believe it. Do you want to talk about it?"

She couldn't truly lie to her mother. "Not yet. I just need time to sort some things out, okay?"

Mother pulled daughter to her feet and surprised Sarah by wrapping her up in a hug. But Sarah was startled for only a moment, and she wasn't too proud to cling to the love and warmth surrounding her.

A short time later, when she finally did pull away, Shauna smoothed Sarah's hair off her face. "When I was pregnant with you and Seth, I had morning sickness for two months. And I had such a craving for home-baked bread and veggies. Tonight, you ate nothing but salad and the cinnamon rolls I baked for dessert."

Sarah's jaw dropped open at the unspoken understanding in her mother's green eyes. She knew. She suspected, at the very least. Would Sarah have that same intuitive connection to her child? Would she know this baby she carried as well as her mother knew her?

She almost formed the words, almost confirmed her mother's suspicion. But she pressed her lips together, instead. Her mother might have guessed she was pregnant, but Sarah wasn't ready to confess who the father was, why he wasn't in her life, or give the answers to any of the questions a mother would ask.

But she could muster a genuine smile. "I'll talk to you soon, Mom. I promise."

"This family has been through a lot together. I love you, Sarah. We all do. We all want you to be safe and happy."

"I know. I love you, too." Feeling a little stronger, a little more sure of herself knowing that she wasn't completely alone in the world, Sarah walked arm in arm with her mom to the front door.

"Call me as soon as you get back to your apartment. If I don't hear from you, I'm sending Eli over." Shauna typed in the code on the security pad to release the alarm and locks. "Better yet, why don't you wait until Eli gets back? Then he can follow you home."

Now it was her turn to offer some reassurance. "I'll be okay. If I know you, the second I leave here, you'll order an extra patrol car to the neighborhood, or something like that, anyway."

Her mother gasped in faux offense. "Would *I* pull strings like that?"

"In a heartbeat." Feeling more like her old self after spending this time with her mother, Sarah smiled a genuine smile. "Give Eli my love."

Fifteen minutes later, Sarah crossed the walkway from the parking garage to her building and pressed the call button for the elevator. Making sure it was empty before stepping in, she pushed the fourth-floor button, then closed her eyes and leaned against the side railing. She was nearly dead on her feet, as much from the stress of the day as from the stress of the pregnancy on her body. When the elevator stopped, she inhaled a reviving breath, opened her eyes and dragged her feet to her apartment door.

The sense that something was wrong hit her as soon as she lifted the latch to her door. The dead bolt had been fastened, but the latch itself was out of place. Had she been in such a sleepy haze this morning that she'd left for school without locking both locks?

Uh-uh. A woman from a cop's family who lived alone didn't make that mistake.

A surge of wary adrenaline left her fully alert as she slid the door open and stepped inside. She pulled her cell phone from her purse as she quickly surveyed the open spaces and sparse furnishings of her loft.

Nothing seemed out of place—nothing was torn up or tossed about as though she'd had a break-in. The television was still there, her CD player and speakers still on the bookshelves. Her laptop was there on the kitchen table.

Maybe she *had* forgotten to lock the door. But Seth had drilled that point into her so hard when she moved out on her own that this would be a first.

No. Something was off.

It was in the air itself—a vaguely familiar scent she couldn't quite identify.

And as Sarah absentmindedly unbuttoned her jacket, she realized how hot it was in the apartment. With the baby growing inside her, her body had fired up some kind of internal furnace, warming her all the way to her fingers and toes in such a way that she kept the thermostat on a cool setting, even at night.

A glance at the thermostat verified that someone had cranked up the heat. That meant someone had been in her apartment. Might still be here.

Sarah didn't bother checking the bathroom or bedroom. She dialed her mom's number and headed for the door. Before she reached it, the furnace klunked and shut itself off. In the silence that followed, Sarah heard another noise. A growl so soft that it was unrecognizable.

"Sarah?" She'd been straining so hard to identify the growling that she jumped at the sound of her mother's voice in her ear. "Did you get home okay? Is everything all right?"

Oh, no. Oh, damn. Not this.

Hurrying straight to the bedroom door, Sarah answered. "Yeah, Mom. I'm home. Sorry, I didn't answer right away. I thought I had a problem with the heat, but I figured it out."

"You're sure?"

"I'm fine. Love you. Good night."

Not growling. Snoring.

Sarah pushed open the bedroom door. Double damn. She pressed her knuckles to her mouth to stifle her curse as the blood inside her drained to her toes, then surged through her veins as anger chased away the threat of danger.

She so did not need to deal with this right now.

This was one problem her mother couldn't help with.

There was a man in her bed.

Chapter Four

"Dad?" Sarah closed in on the man sacked out on top of her bed. His hair was a shade darker than the wrinkled gray suit he wore with its frayed collar turned up around his neck. He huddled inside the summer-weight clothing, arms crossed, knees drawn up, snoring away on her pillow as if he had every right to be there. "Dad!"

He harumphed in his sleep, barely stirring. She snatched up the spare key from her bedside table, taking back what she'd once given him.

"Dad, wake up." Sarah shook him by the shoulder until his eyes blinked open. When he realized who she was, where he was, he swung his feet off the side of the bed and sat up.

"Sarah, sweetie." He smiled and Sarah backed away to avoid the reach of his hand. He pulled his fingers back to scratch at the stubble on his normally clean-shaven jaw. "What, no 'hi' and welcome for your old man?"

"What are you doing here?"

"Catching forty winks." He stood and Sarah moved even farther away, repulsed by the memory of her abused trust in him. Perhaps misreading her displeasure at seeing him, he quickly fixed his collar and smoothed his tie. "Don't worry. I'll sack out on the couch like I did the last time I visited. But I was so tired, I didn't bother looking for pillows and a blanket to make up the sofa bed. I just crashed here."

Sarah shook her head slowly, back and forth, unsure whether it was audacity or indifference that made him so completely oblivious to her shock at seeing him. "You've made yourself right at home, haven't you?"

He made her point by crossing to the foot of the bed and picking up a black nylon locker bag. He set it on the bed, unzipped it and pulled out his shaving kit. "It was freezing in here so I turned up the heat."

"I like it cool—"

"Made myself a sandwich, too, but don't worry—I put the knife and plate I used right into the dishwasher like you told me the last time I was here." When he headed for the bathroom to put away his personal items, Sarah hurried right after him. "Sweetie, why aren't you saying anything? Aren't you glad to see your daddy? You told me I should stop by when I had the chance." He set his kit on the bathroom counter.

She picked it right back up. "That was *before,* Dad."

"Before what?"

She glared at him in the mirror, then spun around and walked away. She dumped the kit into his bag and, without missing a step, picked it up and carried it to the front door. "Before you sold me to Teddy Wolfe."

"What?"

"You can't come here and mooch from me anymore. I finally understand what Seth and Mom have been trying to tell me all along. You're a sick man. Your addiction is all you care about."

"Oh, now don't go believing everything your mother says about me." He snatched her by the elbow, stopping her midstride. "She'll poison you against me."

She jerked away at the sharp flare of anger on his handsome face. "They don't have to say anything. You've disillusioned me all by yourself. There are some things I just can't forgive. And I'm not going to put up with it anymore. I'm done pretending that one day you're going to act like a father again." Sarah tossed his bag into the hall. "Now get out!"

The gears of the restored elevator cranking away at the end of the hallway almost drowned out the hushed shock of his whisper. "I never would have thrown you out of our house."

The hand over his heart added an appropriately over-dramatic effect.

"You'd have to be there first before you could throw anybody out."

"You're picking up Seth's sarcasm," he chided when she slipped past him into the apartment.

"Dad!" His foot was in the door, his shoulder pushing it open as Sarah tried to lock him out. Fine. She'd leave the door open, call the cops—tell them she had an intruder. Sarah turned her back on her father, set the thermostat exactly where she wanted it, then circled into the kitchen to place that call.

Austin Cartwright refused to take the hint. He followed right behind her, crossing his arms and leaning one hip against the counter. It wasn't the first time he'd been in her kitchen, making himself at home and striking up a conversation. But it was the first time Sarah felt cornered in her own home. There was a heaviness in her chest, as though the open walls were closing in, squeezing the available air from her lungs.

"Sarah, sweetie, come on." He was going to try charm now? The lie of it all set her teeth on edge. "As long as the casino is closed, I'm out of work. I lost my apartment. I've got no place to stay. Please. I've always been able to depend on you."

He touched her hand where it rested on the telephone, and Sarah bristled all the way down to her toes. This was the man who'd held her hand when she hadn't made cheerleader in the seventh grade and she'd cried until dinnertime. The same man who'd celebrated with her when she'd made the squad in eighth. The same man who'd set her up for heartbreak and humiliation! And she'd been enough of a sap to not see it coming. "Dad…"

But before she could pull away, he opened her fingers and pressed a shiny silver dollar into her palm. It was the antique coin he kept in his pocket for luck instead of paying bills. "I'm down to my last buck."

She tried not to care that he was homeless. Tried not to feel responsible for taking care of him. The baby growing inside her demanded she be stronger than that. She pushed the coin back into his hand, pushed him away. "Try fast food. Or one of the malls. I'm sure they'll be looking for seasonal help for the coming holidays."

The charm bled from his eyes. "I'm better than part-time work."

"Part-time is better than no work. It's better than

gambling away your career as an architect, gambling away your family. It's better than trying to gamble away Seth's life and using *me* to repay a gambling debt." She raked her fingers through her hair, pulled it free from its ponytail. She took her time adjusting the scrunchie around her wrist just so, buying herself some time so that she could speak without breaking down into tears again. She had to get past the urge to mourn something she'd lost long ago. Her eyes were clear and focused when she looked up at the man who'd sired her some twenty-seven years earlier. "Do you know what Teddy Wolfe wanted? What I did, thinking he cared about me?"

"I don't need to know about your dates." Austin fastened his collar and adjusted his tie, preparing to leave, she hoped. She watched him warily, though, no longer trusting him to do even that. "You said he was hot. That you wanted to get better acquainted with 'James Bond' so you could get out of your rut and live a little. You asked *me* to help speed the process."

"I was a one-night stand. Hell, not even that. More like a half-hour stand. A convenient way to get his rocks off. Then that poor girl was shot. And it was all business as usual for those people at the casino. No one cared about her, and they didn't care about me. Do you have any idea how that made me feel? Any idea how *you* should feel at putting me in that position?"

He turned away to button his jacket, stubbornly heading back toward the kitchen instead of the exit. "I'm sorry you got hurt. I truly am. But he was into you. And you said Teddy's phone calls intrigued you. You asked me to set you up with him. *You* made the choice to have sex with him. I can't help if you're a poor judge of men."

Something broke inside Sarah at that moment— shutting off the guilt, shutting down the love—leaving little to temper the pain and self-recriminations. "Rationalize it any way you want. You knew what kind of man Teddy was, and you didn't even try to warn me. You're a bastard and you used me. You're no father. I wasted years loving you."

He had the gall to look hurt, the temerity to reach out and touch her. "They weren't all bad, were they?"

Sarah slapped his hand away. "Don't do this. Don't give me false hope that anything can ever be right between us again."

His eyes narrowed, gauging the sincerity of her dismissal. "I just need a little help. Until I can get on my feet again."

"Go." She stepped aside to let him pass, showing him she meant what she said. There would be no support, no forgiveness, no love from her corner again.

He took three steps but stopped, grunting with a sound that could have been a laugh or a sigh of regret. He picked up the bottle of big prenatal vitamins that sat on the counter and faced her. "Does your mom know her self-righteous little girl is pregnant?"

Sarah flinched, as though the verbal sucker punch had been a physical counterattack.

"Give me those." She snatched the bottle from his hand and shoved at his chest. "Get out."

"I didn't think so. Maybe we can negotiate some sort of—"

"Get. Out!"

"I believe the lady wants you to leave."

The deep-pitched drawl from the open doorway diverted Austin's attention and stunned Sarah with an audible gasp. *Coop*.

The dark blue eyes were fixed on her father, the front of his camo jacket drawn back to reveal the badge on his belt and the butt of a gun holstered beneath one arm. The urge to run to him jolted through her legs as her volatile emotions registered every reaction to the tall, armed detective. Surprise. Relief. Gratitude. Safety. Attraction.

But she didn't have the right.

And that thunderbolt of awareness dissipated the instant Austin Cartwright wrapped his fingers around her arm and anchored her to his side. Protecting her? Or protecting himself? "I'm Sarah's father. Who the hell are you?"

"I'm KCPD." Cooper's eyes flickered, his gaze dropping to the hand on her arm. His voice still registered easy charm, and the ever-present ball cap indicated his deceptively laid-back humor. But there was nothing but don't-mess-with-me in the length of his stride and carriage of his strong shoulders as he crossed the apartment. "If you paid more attention to your children's lives, you'd know that, Mr. Cartwright." His hand darted out to snatch her father's wrist. Then he did some twisty thing and suddenly Sarah was free and neatly tucked behind Coop's shoulder. Austin cursed and grabbed his wrist, quickly backing away as Coop released him. "I'm Cooper Bellamy, Seth's partner. I'm also a friend of Sarah's."

Friend? After yesterday morning, she was surprised

she rated even that much of a title. She was even more surprised to discover that she clutched a handful of Coop's canvas sleeve in her fist. But was the warmth and strength she felt through layers of cotton a promise she could trust?

Austin massaged his sore wrist. "I have every right to be here."

"Not if the lady says, 'go.'" Coop tilted his head slightly, talking to her while keeping her father in his sights. "You want this man here?"

"No. Dad, please. Just leave."

"Where the hell am I supposed to go?"

"There's a homeless shelter four blocks to the south," Coop suggested. "If you're sober, they'll take you for the night."

"A shelter…?" Sarah saw the wild-eyed desperation in her father's eyes, heard the lonely plea in his voice. "Sarah, sweetie, this is between you and me. Send Bruiser Boy here back to wherever he came from. I'll mind my manners, I promise. I just need your help for a couple of days. There's a Chiefs game this weekend. I can run some numbers—"

"I don't want you here." He thought gambling money was going to fix this? "I can't deal with you right now."

Coop didn't budge. "You heard the lady."

Sad and *needy* blew up into *angry* and *accusing* in the span of a heartbeat. "My wife sent you, didn't she!"

Even after a decade apart, he still refused to get the *ex* prefix right when referring to Sarah's mother.

"Doesn't matter why I'm here. Only that you're leaving."

"This is one huge conspiracy to get me completely out of my daughter's life. Sarah, I love— Who the hell do you think—!"

Austin made the mistake of advancing, and Coop wasted no time twisting him around, pinning his cheek to the counter top and his arm behind his back. "Now… are you gonna walk out of here on your own power, or are we gonna do this the hard way?"

"YOU OKAY?" COOPER LOOKED DOWN to the top of Sarah's head. Her eyes stared at the elevator doors in front of them, her fingers digging into the skin of his forearm.

"He knows about the baby."

Her tension radiated through him, but he determinedly shook it off. Her baby wasn't his concern. "Everyone will sooner or later."

"I was hoping for later." She tilted those green eyes up to him. "You're the only one I've told so far."

Was that an honor or a polite courtesy because the other man she'd slept with was apparently out of the picture? The stigma of knowing she considered *their* morning together a mistake twisted in his gut.

Cooper needed some distance. He pried Sarah's fingers from the sleeve of his jacket. Her skin was cool to the touch, but her grip was rock-solid. Despite his initial scare that he'd heard raised voices and found her apartment door propped wide open, she was all right.

The baby, too, he supposed, his gaze drawn to the hand she rested over her abdomen.

You don't care about that, he warned himself.

All the Cartwright women had received threats, according to the alert he'd gotten from Captain Kincaid. And, yeah, having secrets and a soft heart around a user like Austin Cartwright was bound to cause trouble somewhere along the line. Cut off from the rest of the world the way Sarah's apartment seemed to be, this could have been disastrous.

But not tonight. Tonight, Sarah and her baby were safe.

He could put that in his report to Captain Kincaid, and ignore the sense of relief that same information gave him on a personal level. *You don't care.* The elevator doors had closed on Austin Cartwright and the obsessive demands he tried to make on his daughter. It was time to put things into perspective between him and Sarah.

She was a citizen of Kansas City and he was a cop, protecting her from an unwelcome trespasser.

Nothing more to it.

Coop gave her a nudge toward her apartment. "Go back inside and bolt the door. I'll be right out here in case your dad comes back—or anyone else stops by to pay an unwanted visit."

"You're going to camp out here in the hallway?"

"I don't think spending the night on your couch is a good idea."

"Ouch."

The shadows framing her upturned eyes nearly made him forget his resolve to keep his distance. It was too tempting to want to hold her—to comfort her, to kiss her. And that didn't say much for his male pride to still be wanting a woman who'd slept with him on the rebound from another man. So he purposely turned and eyed the wooden bench between the two potted silk palms near the elevator. It was too short to stretch out on and too hard to even want to, but it would serve its purpose. "It's not so bad. There's a place to sit. Good vantage point to keep an eye on the elevator and the stairwell door. What more could a man ask for?"

"It's ridiculous that you're staying at all." She hadn't moved one step closer to her door. "You should go on home, Coop. I'll be fine."

"Those aren't my orders."

Her eyes blazed with an emerald fire. She crossed her arms, prickling up like a banty hen. "Great. Did Seth call you to come babysit me?"

Coop could honestly answer no to that one.

"My mother?" The fire died and one arm drifted down to include the baby in her shielding posture. "They think I'm the helpless one in the family, don't they?"

"They think you're the one who lives alone. Unprotected. Without even so much as a neighbor to go to if you need some help." Coop thumbed over his shoulder to the vacant apartment across the hall from Sarah's. "Look, I come from a big family, so I can appreciate how you'd like a quiet place to get away from it all— especially after spending the day with ten-year-olds. But let's face it, this isn't the safest place to be."

"Just because I couldn't get rid of my dad doesn't mean I'm in danger here."

"What if someone more dangerous had been in your apartment, and I hadn't stopped by?" Judging by the color that blanched from her cheeks, his point was made. But scaring Sarah didn't feel like any kind of victory. Coop pulled off his cap and smoothed his palm over the top of his head before turning the bill toward his collar and putting it back on. Maybe the goofy fashion choice would look a little less threatening and she'd actually listen to him. "Look, between KCPD's investigation, Teddy's death and you witnessing that murder, your family has had some pretty heavy run-in's with Wolfe International. I wouldn't put it past Theodore Wolfe to want to exact some kind of payback from any one of you."

She pulled her shoulders back, determinedly adding strength to all five feet of her. "It was just a note. And none of you can prove it was even from Wolfe. Besides, from the description my students gave, the man who walked up to the playground couldn't have been that old."

"He's the head of an organized crime family. He's not going to do the actual footwork himself. Don't blow this off just to prove your independence to your family."

"Fine. I'm warned. I'll be more careful."

"Did that note scare you?" Her gaze dropped to the center of his chest and her arms hugged tighter. "Yeah, I thought so."

"For the kids. I was scared for my kids at school." The fire was back. "But damn it, Coop—if Mom's going to assign someone to watch my back, it shouldn't be you."

"Talk about 'ouch.'"

"I don't mean you can't do the job." She reached out, but quickly pulled her hand away. *Right.* Touching wasn't a good idea. "I mean you shouldn't have to. It isn't fair to you considering our history."

History. Apt way of putting those forbidden feelings that he'd foolishly given in to that morning.

"You're feeling sorry for me?" Man, this woman was tough on the ego. Bristling, Coop straightened, towering over her in the empty hallway. "I outgrew the need for anybody's pity a long time ago."

"It's not pity. I just… Look, I appreciate you helping me with Dad tonight. And that thing you did, with just your hands was…amazing." She splayed her fingers in the air like a magician, then just as quickly drew her fists back over her heart. "But I'm probably the last person you want to be around right now. So, go home. I promise I'll lock my door, and—"

"Trust me, Sarah. I'm a big boy. You don't have to worry about my feelings." He had to explain to her— he needed to hear it for himself—that his being here tonight was all about protecting and serving the people of Kansas City. Nothing more. Nothing personal. Watching over Sarah Cartwright wasn't a habit he intended to get into. Being there for her wasn't a responsibility he was entitled to in any way. "It's the middle of my shift. I'll stay here until B shift comes on in the morning. Then there'll be another officer here to replace me. He'll keep an eye on your apartment. Plus, we'll assign someone to assist the school patrolman while you're at work, in case the guy with the notes shows his face there again. I'll be sure to introduce you so you know the names and faces you can trust."

"I see." She curled her arms around her middle again, and Coop itched with the need to provide that hug for her. But what would be the point? The sooner he got over her, the easier life would be. "So, back there, when you told my dad we were still friends, that was just for his benefit. You're only here because it's your job. My stupid choices hurt you that much?"

"I don't know how I feel, Sarah. But you have other priorities right now that are more important than some relationship that was never gonna happen for us, anyway. You've always wanted something I couldn't give you. And I'm not just talking about my little Coopers. You wanted excitement. Adventure. Something different than the world of cops and rules you've always known. Hell, maybe you just wanted a full head of hair."

"I'm sorry. I wish this baby was—"

"It's not." When she would have reached out to him to offer some other apology, he took her by the arm and walked her to her door. "Don't worry about me. I'll work through it—get past it. I'd never be able to explain to Seth that I boinked his sister without asking his permission first, anyway." He deposited her inside the door and let her go. "In the meantime I'll do my job."

"Boinked?"

He could see how his choice of words hurt her. Hell, it hurt him to say it. But it got the job done by ending all this touchy-feely, hey-we-made-a-mistake-so-let's-talk-it-out stuff. *I'm sorry* weren't the words he'd always fantasized about hearing from her. "Good night, Sarah."

As he pulled the door shut, he heard her soft whisper from the other side. "Good night."

He waited until he heard the dead bolt lock into place. He waited until he finally heard her footsteps moving away from the door. He waited until he heard the sounds of her working in the kitchen, maybe fixing a late-night snack before going to bed. Then he turned and braced himself for a long, solitary, uncomfortable night on that bench. A cup of coffee would be nice.

Hell, getting past this kick-in-the-gut reaction every time he thought about another man's baby growing inside her belly would be even nicer.

It should have been his. Sarah Cartwright should have been his. But she didn't want him, except maybe as a friend. And he wasn't sure he could go back to that.

The seat was even lower to the floor than he'd anticipated. He settled his hips on the rock-hard wood, leaned his back against the wall and stretched his legs out in front of him, trying to make himself fit.

He was having about as much success with that as he'd had trying to fit into Sarah's life.

Oh yeah, even without the bench, this was going to be a hell of a long night.

IT WAS A CRIME TO LOOK as pretty and perky as Sarah Cartwright did, dressed and ready for school the next morning, when Cooper felt like a twisted-up pretzel. But the cup of coffee she brought out in a travel mug helped revive him a little.

"It's not a peace offering," she insisted, referring to his don't-pity-me speech the night before. "I think it's just common decency to offer a man a cup of coffee in the morning. Besides, the doctor said I should watch my caffeine. But I do love the smell of it, so you gave me the excuse to brew some."

"You have heard of decaf?" Coop asked, feeling some of his humor returning.

She adjusted the book bag on her shoulder and

pressed the elevator's call button. "First thing on my shopping list when I get a chance to go to the store after school today."

Coop waited beside her while the gears of the old elevator brought the car up to the fourth floor. A closer look at her pale skin revealed she wasn't as perky as her good-morning smile might have indicated. Either she'd had another bout of morning sickness or she hadn't slept any better than he had—starting at every unidentified noise, or torturing himself with might-have-beens and recriminations.

Coop walked her straight to her car and locked her inside. Then he followed her in his truck through town to West Lawn Elementary, where he handed off his watch to Mickey Sandoval. The young Latino officer was all smiles and reassurances as Coop introduced him to Sarah and her principal. Then Sandoval left with Abe Stern, the uniformed officer who taught the school's Drug Abuse Resistance Education (D.A.R.E.) program and provided campus security, to familiarize himself with the building and grounds and acquaint himself with the students so they wouldn't report Mickey as a stranger.

As for Sarah, there were no more apologies, no goodbyes. A trio of students surrounded her before she even got through the door to her classroom. Both the kids and teacher alike lit up with the lively interchange regarding social studies projects and presentation plans.

Coop's mouth curved with a half smile. He wasn't too sure that Sarah had gotten past the shock of being pregnant yet to have truly bonded with the baby and think about future plans. But he had no doubt that she would be a natural in the motherhood department. At every stage of the game—from newborn to energetic preteens like this crew, to the angst and drama that lay beyond. She was smart. Intuitive. Compassionate. She'd make a great mom. She deserved the chance to be that mom.

Coop ran his hand over his stubbled jaw, wiping away his grin. That was one of the reasons why he'd kept his distance from Sarah in the past—because he wouldn't deny her the one thing he couldn't give her. But the desire for her—the desire to share a life with her—stirred inside him even now. He'd help raise his younger brothers and sisters. He was a bona fide pal and babysitter extraordinaire to his friends' kids—like the assistant D.A.'s son and adopted grandson, Dalton and Tyler Powers. But he wasn't sure it was right to love a woman like Sarah without worrying that she had sacrificed something too precious to be with him. With adoption or foster kids or getting involved with the students at her school, they could share in caring for a child. But how strong would their love have to be to get past that sacrifice always lurking in the background?

Sarah might care about him on some level. She might even be attracted to him. But, judging by her reaction to him after that morning together, and in the months of silence that followed, she wasn't in love with him. Telling him about her pregnancy had been an obligation she felt she owed him—not a celebration she'd hoped to share. It made for a lousy start to a relationship between him and Sarah, and with guilt and regret pecking away at it, that relationship would probably be doomed. But denying Sarah the opportunity to love and raise a child of her own would be like denying him the medical treatment that had saved his life. Even if the child wasn't his, Coop could never begrudge her that.

After sending the students out to the playground to wait for the morning bell, Sarah went into her classroom to prepare for the day and Coop climbed back into his truck. He was beat, but he had time for a shave and a shower and a short nap before he had to report for duty at the precinct.

Coop was wrapped in a towel, shaving away the shadow that valiantly tried to grow around the back of his head, when his cell phone rang. Making a face at the weary reflection in the bathroom mirror, he walked into the bedroom to pick up the call.

"Bellamy."

"Hey, I hear you spent the night with my sister." Seth. Yikes. The lingering heat from his shower quickly dissipated as Coop squirmed at the unintentional double entendre of that greeting. But it was a thank-you for last night, not an accusation about anything else. "I owe you one, man."

"Just add it to the list." Coop peeled the towel off his hips and slipped into his shorts and jeans, needing a little more coverage to keep his wits about him and not give anything away. "Are you and Rebecca okay?"

"Yeah. We had a serious…conversation…last night, about staying safe."

"Was that *conversation* anything like lunch the other day?"

He could easily imagine Seth's answering smile. "I've got a man watching her at the paper, and she promised not to do any field investigating until we track down the source of the threats."

"Do you really have any doubts about the source?"

"None. Wolfe's behind this. But without any proof, all we can do is watch and wait and pray he's not going to make good on them."

I'm coming for you.

I'm coming for everyone you love.

But you won't see me until it's too late.

Yeah. They needed to do a lot of praying.

Coop toweled off the remaining dollops of shaving cream and returned to the bathroom to throw the towel over its hook. "Sandoval's taken over my watch so I can get some sleep. Kincaid's promised an officer dedicated to your sister around the clock."

"Kincaid's a good man. With you keeping tabs on Sarah and Eli watching Mom around the clock, I won't worry."

"Seth Cartwright won't worry?" Cooper scoffed. He knew his buddy better than that. "Then what are you gonna do with your time?"

"Fine, smart-ass. So I won't worry *as much*."

Though Seth would surely guess there was more to the story, Coop needed to have a serious moment. "About Sarah—and watching her. Normally, I don't mind doing you or your mom a favor, but…" A strident ring from the telephone beside his bed interrupted his plea for reassignment. That was either lousy timing or a stroke of luck. "Hey, man. I've got another call on the landline." Telling Seth that spending so much time with his sister was a hardship for him would have to wait. He needed a clearer, rested brain to explain why, anyway. So he ended the call. "Catch you later."

"Will do."

Coop smiled when he read the caller ID indicating the younger of his two sisters. "Gracie. What's up?"

"Mom said I could give you a call." The clicks and beeps he heard in the background told him his athletic sister was home for lunch, fueling up on popcorn or some other snack from the microwave before she finished her afternoon classes and went to volleyball practice after school. "Uncle Walt called last night. He says we're all invited to his place south of St. Louis for Thanksgiving this year. Do you know if you have to work then?"

"No clue yet, kiddo. But if I know Walt, the invitation means he's got some newfangled way to cook a turkey he wants to try out on us. You sure you want to be a guinea pig?"

Grace popped a bite of something into her mouth and chewed around her words. "Maybe. But he says he's done some fun stuff with his lake cabin, too, that he wants to show us. Maybe he put in a Jacuzzi, or souped up his boat."

Coop laughed at the idea of speed-boating or water-skiing on a cold lake with the onset of winter in Missouri. "You'd be happy if he'd install a telephone line so you and Clint can play your computer games."

"O-oh. You think that's what he did?"

"Who knows?" The lovable old coot who'd stepped in as a grandpa figure when his younger brother—

Coop's father—had died, was a retired geology professor from the University of Missouri. Part mad scientist and part Indiana Jones, Walt gave new meaning to the term *family character,* with his explorations and experiments and ongoing quest for learning. "But it does sound mighty intriguing. I'll see what I can do about getting Thanksgiving weekend off."

"Cool. Well, I need to get back to school. I'll tell Mom you said hi."

"Give her a hug for me."

"Bye."

Coop had barely hung up when his cell phone rang again. What was this, Grand Central Station? Maybe he'd better get back into the shower so he could have some peace and quiet.

He didn't recognize the number, but answered anyway. "Bellamy."

"Mickey Sandoval."

Coop braced, expecting bad news. "Is something wrong at West Lawn?"

"Nah, everything's cool here, man." Sandoval quickly reported that it was business as usual at the school. There'd been no unidentified visitors, and Sarah had done nothing more unusual than sneak a few bites of a granola bar when her students left for P.E. class.

"That's all well and good, but why are you calling me?" Coop's eyes narrowed, as if he could assess the young detective's intentions by studying the tan henley shirt lying over the foot of the bed. "You should be reporting to Kincaid."

"Oh." Sandoval sounded surprised. "I thought she was something special to you, man."

Ah, crap. His mixed-up feelings regarding Sarah weren't so obvious that a relative stranger could spot them, were they? "Commissioner Cartwright called and asked me to check on her last night," was the easiest excuse.

"Yeah. I know she's the commish's daughter. It'd be our badges if anything happened to her, right? And if we play it right, I bet there's a commendation or raise for us in it, too."

Coop shifted on his feet, growing a little edgy at the younger detective's materialistic motivation. "She's the material witness in a murder investigation, and she's received an unspecified threat. You need to keep a close eye on her for that reason. Not for your Christmas bonus."

"Hey, it's all cool, man. I know how to do my job. I'll call Kincaid as soon as I get back from lunch."

"You're leaving?"

"Relax. Abe will be with her. Do you want to talk to him? Or her?"

"No." Coop knew it made sense for one cop to spell another so they could take breaks and stay sharp. But he just had a feeling that Mickey Sandoval wasn't as dedicated to guarding Sarah as he'd like him to be. "Call me as soon as you're back from lunch and back on the job."

"I thought you wanted me to report to Kincaid."

"Just call."

Coop pressed the disconnect button before he added something inappropriately territorial like he'd be holding the detective personally accountable should anything happen to Sarah while he took off for lunch.

He tossed the phone onto the bed and pulled on his insulated shirt, tucking it in with a little more force than cotton knit called for. By the time he'd buttoned his denim shirt over it and tied on his shoes, he was chanting a mantra of advice.

Walk away, Coop. The sanest thing he could do was just walk away.

He couldn't be close to Sarah Cartwright without wanting her, without worrying about her, without blaming her for not needing him in the same way he needed her. He couldn't be her friend, couldn't be her protector—not when he couldn't think straight around her. Getting pregnant by someone else wasn't her fault, especially since the guy didn't have the cojones to stick around and make the relationship work. Gone was the best place for that jackass to be, as far as Coop was concerned.

But why had she turned to another man for sex and a fling when Cooper's arms had been waiting for her all along?

Because he was another big brother? The sidekick? The comic relief? Because he wasn't man enough for her?

How could making love with her feel so perfect, while *loving* her just messed up his head?

"Walk away, Coop."

He slipped his arms into his holster and clipped on his badge. Forget taking a nap. He needed to get to work. He needed to immerse himself in a stack of boring reports or run some interviews or pull over a jaywalker. Something to keep him busy. Something he could be objective about. Something to give himself a means to salvage his battered pride.

Something that could make him forget that he loved Sarah Cartwright.

Because she didn't love him.

Chapter Five

A stack of mind-numbing paperwork later, Cooper and Seth were walking out of the Fourth Precinct offices. Though they'd traded see-you-tomorrows and chatted up weekend plans with the desk sergeant when they'd checked out, Coop was deep in thought as they strolled down the sidewalk and headed for the open air parking lot that was kitty-corner from the building.

He was pensive enough that Seth pointed it out. "Either you're coming down with the flu, or you've got something eatin' at you. Cooper Bellamy having a quiet day means something ain't right with the world."

With Sandoval's comment about making brownie points with the commissioner still nagging at him, Coop wanted a little more time to think about whether or not he could handle being on Sarah's detail before he told her family he wasn't up for the job. Coop buried his hands in his pockets and shrugged off Seth's concern. "It can wait."

The streetlights were coming on early as they waited for a break in rush-hour traffic to jog across the street. But Seth wouldn't let it drop. "Is everything okay at home? Sisters? Brothers? Mom? We've been a little obsessed with my family and concerns lately—and you've backed me up every step of the way. One of these days you're gonna have to let me return the favor."

Coop mustered a grin. "One of these days."

Seth gave Coop's arm a light smack, stopping them from splitting up to head for their separate vehicles. "Is it work? We can go grab a beer if something's buggin' you."

Normally as intense as a prize fighter in the opening round, it was hard to miss when Seth Cartwright was expressing genuine concern. All the more reason to avoid this conversation right now. Coop mustered a grin and deftly switched the topic to send him on his way. "You don't want to grab a beer with me. Not when you've got Miss Stilts waiting for you at the *Journal.* You'd better pick up Rebecca before she ditches the man watching her and decides to investigate the source of those notes without you."

"She *is* kind of an independent thinker that way, isn't she? I suppose you're right."

But Seth was no fool. He'd stay on Coop's case until he got an explanation that made sense. "Maybe tomorrow or Saturday I'll take you up on that beer."

"It's a deal." The two shook hands and Coop headed farther down the sidewalk toward his truck while Seth pulled out the keys to his car. Mr. Intensity shouted after Coop. "Hey—what do you mean, *Miss Stilts?* You been lookin' at my fiancée's legs?"

Coop personally preferred a particular short and sleek pair, but that wasn't what this verbal sparring was about. He glanced over his shoulder and shouted back, "You can't miss them—they're a mile long!"

"You find a girl of your own and keep your eyes on—"

A flash of light bloomed beneath the hood of Seth's car. He turned to run, but there was no place for him to go. In a span of milliseconds that ticked off like eons, an explosion lifted the car off its axles and blew it into a million pieces. A fusillade of shrapnel caught Seth from behind and knocked him to the pavement.

"Seth!"

His partner was down. Out cold. Bleeding.

Coop ran. He dragged Seth's limp body beyond the reach of the flames engulfing the car. He checked for a pulse. Said a prayer and got on his phone while others rushed to help. "Officer down. I need a bus in the southeast parking lot outside the Fourth Precinct Building on East Linwood."

Shielding Seth from the fire's intense heat and drifting debris by peeling off his jacket and draping it over his partner's lacerated back and legs, Coop swept the area with his gaze. He couldn't find what he was looking for. Someone running. Laughing. Smiling with satisfaction. This wasn't any random act of sabotage.

Some of his fellow officers were already moving vehicles away from the fire, clearing spectators to a safer distance, managing traffic. Coop snapped his fingers and called over the closest man. "Search this area. It didn't blow when he unlocked the door. That means the bomb was on a timer or a remote detonator. The perp could still be close by."

The blue suit nodded, grabbed his partner and radioed in the order to sweep the area.

The dispatcher on the line requested information and advised him that an ambulance and fire engine were on the way. "This is Cooper Bellamy, detective, Fourth Precinct. I've got a car explosion and fire. It matches an M.O. used by fugitive Shaw McDonough. No sighting of him in the area as of yet. But I repeat. Officer down. Get me that bus. Now."

COOPER HUNG BACK at the fringe of the family and friends circling around Seth Cartwright's hospital bed.

The lights had been dimmed to accommodate the strain on Seth's vision as he dealt with the effects of a concussion and the surgery to remove shards of metal and glass from his back and legs. Wounds had been cleaned, gashes stitched, nerve and muscle reactions checked and monitored, burns treated, and a cast had been set around a leg that had been broken by the impact of one particularly nasty chunk of shrapnel.

Though he lay on his stomach on a special bed, Seth's thoughts were reassuringly clear, and his groggy voice answered every question and comment with his typical dry wit.

Their Fourth Precinct captain, Mitch Taylor, had joined Captain Kincaid from the task force to convey the department's concern and offer their support in whatever way the family needed. "So the doc says you're gonna live, Cartwright."

"Yes, sir. Can't say how everything's gonna work for a few days, but the bastards haven't gotten me yet."

"Seth, don't talk like that." Though Coop's direct view was blocked, there was no mistaking the hushed reprimand in Rebecca Page's voice. "I don't want anyone getting you. Except me."

"It's okay, sweetheart. That's just tough talk so the pain knows not to mess with me. But it's your turn to watch my back for a while now, hmm?"

"You know I will." The moment of silence and gentle ribbing and laughs that followed indicated that there was probably some kind of kiss. Coop dropped his chin to his chest and grinned. The man was down and out, but he could still get some.

The only other person in the room holding Seth's hand as tightly as Rebecca was Seth's mother, Shauna. She assumed both maternal and departmental authority by clearing her throat. "I think we'd better let Seth get some sleep. The doctor says he needs his rest before they come back to run more tests in the morning."

There was a chorus of "Yes, ma'am's" and "Ah, Mom," handshaking and a few more kisses.

Eli Masterson stepped forward and wrapped an arm around his wife's waist. "When the boss lady says to clear a room, we move out. Gentlemen? Ladies?"

"I love you, Seth." That was Sarah's voice, soft and sure. Coop straightened, remembering that same sweet mouth saying, *Hold me. Kiss me.* He believed in the tight bond she shared with her brother. Could the need behind the words she'd spoken to him that day be just as real? Could his instincts have been so far off that day? Or had she been just so upset by witnessing a murder that she didn't know what she'd wanted from him?

Sarah hooked her arm through Eli's and walked past on the opposite side from her mom, conveniently or purposely avoiding him. A few fellow cops, A.J. Rodriguez and Josh Taylor, followed. Then came the captains.

"Take care, buddy. We'll try to keep the world running without you on the job for a while." After shaking Seth's hand, Cooper fell in behind them to give his partner the peace and quiet he needed.

"Thanks. I love that knack of yours for being where you need to be."

Rebecca nodded. "The doctor said the burns would have been a lot worse if you hadn't pulled him away from the fire."

Coop offered the statuesque brunette a hug of her own. "Hey, I wouldn't do it for just anybody."

"Well, I'm glad you were there. I just figured out how to let somebody into my life again—" she smiled down at Seth before kissing his cheek "—and I don't want to lose him now."

Shrugging off the gratitude, Coop grinned. "Like I told Pee-Wee here, I'm keeping tabs on what he owes me. Payback's gonna be pretty special. I'm thinking something along the lines of—"

"Detective Bellamy." Uh-oh, that was Mama at the door. "Seth needs his sleep."

Coop nodded to the commissioner. "Yes, ma'am." He winked at Rebecca. "You take care of him. Later, Seth."

"Hey, Coop, hang on. I need to talk to you a sec." Seth squeezed Rebecca's hand, then dragged it to his lips for a kiss. "Do you mind, Bec?"

Though Rebecca clearly didn't want to leave his side,

she seemed to understand that Seth wouldn't rest until he'd said whatever he wanted to say to Coop. She nodded and picked up a washcloth and cup from beside the bed. "I'll go get some more of the crushed ice you liked. But I'll be back."

"I'm counting on it." But the smile Seth gave her faded behind a weary sigh the instant she left the room. "I need to ask you a favor."

"Sure." Coop knelt beside the bed to put himself on eye level with his partner. "Name it. Anything."

There was nothing to joke about in the seriousness of Seth's bruised expression. "I need you to keep an eye on Sarah for me."

Anything but that.

But Coop bit his tongue. Seth had more to say. "Mom's a cop, she carries a gun and she knows what to look for. Besides, Eli watches over her like a guard dog. Rebecca's with me here, and we've got round-the-clock protection. But Sarah's on her own. And she's such an innocent about the world—you know, trusting people she shouldn't, expecting the best out of others you can't count on—like my dad."

Had Seth really talked to his sister lately? She'd grown up beyond the wide-eyed innocent he was describing.

Still, with a baby in her belly and a murderer she could identify loose somewhere in the world, she was plenty vulnerable in other ways.

Seth squeezed his eyes shut, as though pain or fatigue or both were finally getting the better of him. "Looks like I'll be out of commission for a few days." A few days was how long the surgeon who'd worked on him said he'd be confined to his hospital bed. Seth would be lucky if he was able to get dressed and walk up the aisle under his own power by his Christmas Eve wedding date. "I wouldn't trust anyone else with the job but you, buddy."

Coop hesitated. He'd just determined that he needed to keep his distance from Sarah or he was bound to get burned. Protecting her would mean anything but distance. "Captain Kincaid has already ordered a round-the-clock watch on your family. Sarah isn't alone."

Seth's eyes opened with a frown. "You got a problem with this? I thought you loved her the way I do."

"I—" He couldn't say it. He couldn't lie to his partner about his mixed-up feelings for Sarah. But he couldn't tell him the truth, either.

A bit of Irish temper roused Seth onto his elbows. He grunted with the pain and effort. "You know how the bureaucracy works, Coop. There may be a man assigned to Sarah, but I want someone around her who *cares* that she's safe. Who won't get distracted by a coffee break or some other sweet thing walking by."

"Easy. Easy." Coop sprang to his feet and urged Seth back onto the bed. The fact that he had to take most of his partner's muscular weight to ease him back to a relatively comfortable position told Coop just how weakened Seth was right now. He smoothed the light hair off his partner's forehead and reached for Seth's hand, his decision made. "I care. No joke, buddy. Your sister is…special to me. You heal. I'll keep Sarah safe."

The tension in Seth relaxed. "Thanks."

"I'll protect her like she was my own." They shook

hands, sealing the deal. Coop couldn't walk away now. He'd given his word. "I promise."

COOP LISTENED TO MAC TAYLOR'S preliminary report over the telephone. As commander of the KCPD crime lab's day shift, the scientist-turned-cop would already have some of the answers Coop needed tonight.

"Obviously, it will take us days—even weeks—to sort through the debris from the explosion to get all the facts, but, yes, our findings thus far indicate the bomb was triggered by a remote detonator."

Coop nodded as he strolled down the hallway of St. Luke's Hospital toward Seth's room. His midnight cup of coffee had revived him enough to get the ball rolling on his own investigation into the attempt on his partner's life. "So it's the same type of explosion that took out Rebecca Page's car when she was investigating Wolfe International?"

"It appears so." Ever the scientist who made decisions based on facts instead of hunches, though, Mac added, "It's too soon to say conclusively that both bombs were set by the same perp, just that the M.O. matches. Whoever planted both charges had to be close enough to the crime scene to spot his target before pushing the button. So, yes, it was a deliberate attack. But he could have been randomly targeting a member of KCPD, not necessarily Seth."

Coop didn't buy the random theory, not when members of Seth's family had already received threats.

Coop rounded the corner and spotted said family—Sarah, her mother and Eli—as well as Rebecca and a uniformed officer in the waiting room area. *One of the doctors must be in the room with Seth right now.* Coop ducked back out of sight, not quite ready to put on his good-ol'-boy persona for Seth's loved ones.

He dropped the volume of his voice and asked Mac the most important question of all. "Do you think Shaw McDonough could be the bomber?"

"I thought McDonough had disappeared out of the country."

"*Could* it be him?" Coop repeated.

"Well, he used to be Theodore Wolfe's enforcer. He reputedly could handle a gun, knife or bomb with equal skill. But to be honest..." Coop braced for the rebuttal. "We don't have concrete proof that McDonough even set the first bomb. And without a gun to match ballistics to, I don't have the forensics to back up the eyewitness's testimony that says he shot Dawn Kingsley. McDonough might just be an easy scapegoat, and there's somebody even more dangerous—because we don't suspect him—out there. Maybe it's someone who works for Wolfe, maybe not."

Comforting words. *Like hell.*

But at least Mac's report made sense. "Thanks, Mac. Keep me posted when you know more."

"I will."

Coop disconnected the call and clipped the phone back onto his belt. His promise to Seth was getting more daunting by the moment. And not just for personal reasons. How did he protect Sarah from a threat when there was no tangible proof who that threat was or where it was coming from?

The elevator doors at the end of the hallway opened, and out walked at least one threat Coop could identify.

He pulled away from the wall where he'd been leaning, charged with a new energy as he strode down the corridor to greet Austin Cartwright.

Though it was natural for a father—even an estranged one—to want to visit his injured son in the hospital, there was nothing natural about the dramatic transformation in Austin's appearance. He was in far better shape than the last time Coop had seen him. Sarah's father sported a new suit, new haircut and even a dab of aftershave, if he wasn't mistaken. And the oversize potted plant he carried hadn't come cheap.

Coop planted his feet and braced his hands on his hips, blocking Austin's path. "So how did that shelter work out for you, Mr. Cartwright?"

"Detective Bellamy." Austin frowned through a controlled inhale and exhale. So the old man *did* know who he was. "I got me a new job now. No thanks to you."

"Doing what?"

"I'm consulting." Yeah, that answer was vague enough to be suspicious. Knowing Austin, he'd probably consulted with a bookie and had gotten lucky for a change. "You tell Sarah that. I landed on my feet without her help. Though a hug and a show of support wouldn't have killed her, would it?"

Cooper wasn't sure of the entire Cartwright family history, but if Sarah didn't want her father around, then tonight of all nights, he wasn't going to stay. "Feel free to leave anytime."

"Just what is your relationship with my daughter,

Bellamy? I believe you're taking liberties you have no right to. You're lucky I don't sue you for police brutality."

Sue away. "Your son almost got killed today. If the way you treat your daughter is any indication, then the rest of your family doesn't need to deal with you right now."

"Hey, you two." Cooper jumped at the brush of Sarah's hand against his back. "This is a hospital, remember? They tend to prefer quiet voices around here."

Though he quickly masked his startled reaction to her touch by moving aside and letting her join them, Coop was already silently cursing his incompetence. Great. He hadn't heard her sneaking up behind him. So far he was doing a real whiz-bang job of looking out for her. He positioned himself directly behind Sarah, ready to back her up in whatever way she might need. "Your father was just leaving."

"I think that's up to her," Austin insisted.

Sarah's mouth curved into a rueful smile. "Thanks for coming by, Dad. I know somewhere, deep down inside, Seth will appreciate it. But the doctors are with him right now, and then he needs to rest. None of us can see him until tomorrow morning."

"Is he going to be okay?"

"Eventually. The doctors are worried about blood clots and infection, but so far, everything seems to be under control."

"My boy's a fighter." Coop tried to gauge the sincerity of Austin's concern. But with a practiced liar, it was hard to tell. "I know I haven't done right by you, sweetie. But there's not a day that goes by I don't think about you and Seth and your mom."

"I know that, Dad. I know you don't mean to hurt us." The stiff set of Sarah's shoulders indicated she was tolerating, if not necessarily buying into her father's words. "But you still do."

"Ah, sweetie—I can make it up to you. Just give me a chance."

"You've had plenty of chances. I think it's best if you just go now. Before you upset Mom or Seth."

Or Sarah, Coop wanted to add.

"Okay. I understand. I'll try again another time. Thanks for talking to me, sweetie."

"Sure."

But when Austin moved to hug her, she backed into Coop's chest and he willingly let one hand slide to her waist while he reached over her shoulder to block Austin's approach.

"Back off."

There was a flare of something wild and hateful in Austin's eyes before he nodded and retreated. Once he was beyond arm's reach, Coop dropped his hand to settle with possessive familiarity on the other side of Sarah's waist. He might have imagined the way she curled more securely into the wall of his chest.

With his touch rebuffed, Austin held out the plant instead. "Will you give this to Seth? There's a note attached."

"Sure." Sarah accepted the gift from her father, carefully shifting her grip to avoid even accidentally brushing against his fingers. "Good night, Dad."

"Tell your brother I tried to see him." Austin backed away. He waited for one of the cleaning crew to pass by them before he added, "You take care of yourself. And the little one."

Coop felt the flinch in Sarah's posture, and in an unconsciously protective gesture, slid his hand down to cover hers where she'd moved it to shield her belly behind the plant. "Good night, Mr. Cartwright."

"Detective."

As Austin turned and headed for the elevator, Sarah's fingers twisted and laced together with Coop's, holding on to him, holding him close. The subtle plea for support, the silent symbol of the alliance they'd once shared, reached deep into Cooper's soul, trying to speak of what was right and what should be. And, for a moment, he gave in to that connection they shared. He dipped his lips to the crown of her hair and let his body circle around her as she turned her cheek into his shoulder and shared the embrace.

"I've gotcha," he whispered against the thick wheaten silk of her hair. "I've gotcha both."

The distinct clearing of a female throat startled them both, and Sarah moved away with such an embarrassing hurry that Coop had to catch the potted green plant before it hit the floor.

"Hey, Mom." Sarah's cheeks were flushed with color when she peeked around Seth's shoulder to greet her mother. "Did you see…?" She glanced back at the elevator doors.

"I saw. Looks like your father's horse must have come in. I haven't seen him looking like that for months." She drew her gaze back to her daughter. "What did he mean, take care of 'the little one'?"

"Um—"

Sarah fumbled, but Coop easily stepped in to answer. "That's his nickname for me, apparently. You know, like calling the fat guy 'Slim.'"

"I get it." Shauna nodded, accepting his answer, lame as it was. She seemed to give them both a knowing look before stretching up on tiptoe to kiss Coop's cheek. "Thank you for saving my son's life. And thank you for being my daughter's friend. Here. I'll take that." She pulled the plant from Coop's hands. "If Seth doesn't want it, we'll donate it to someone in the hospital who needs some cheering up." She reached out and cupped the curve of Sarah's cheek. "You be sure to get some rest tonight, too. You look exhausted."

"I will, Mom."

Coop and Sarah stood there, side by side, waiting until Shauna disappeared around the corner. When Coop glanced down at Sarah's pale expression, he could see she looked about as uneasy as he felt. "Are you sure she doesn't know about the baby?"

Sarah tucked her hair behind her ears, then resolutely tipped her chin. "She's a mom and the commissioner. She's got that look down pat. If she acts like she already knows something, then we're more likely to open up and start talking about things, giving her the information she wants." Her green gaze tilted up to his. "But, no, I haven't told her I'm pregnant or about what we…what *I* did." She nodded toward the hallway where her brother lay, broken and bloody and fighting for his life. "Mom has enough stress right now without worrying over me."

"That's what moms do. You'll learn that soon enough."

In the awkward silence that followed, Sarah rubbed at her tummy. "I'm starting to feel that way already. And I can't even feel it moving inside me yet. Just some little flutters, if I use my imagination." Sarah laughed, a sound Coop hadn't heard for a long time. "Then again, maybe it's just gas."

Flutters? Like life moving, growing inside her? What he wouldn't give to have shared that miracle with her. His fingers uncurled with the wish to touch her there again, too—to share, even in some small way—that miracle growing inside her.

"I'm sure it's not gas." But the urge to laugh didn't come. Instead, images of Teddy Wolfe's dead body and of the passport photo and composite drawing used to I.D. Shaw McDonough blipped through Cooper's mind.

The baby wasn't his. Sarah wasn't his. Not if she didn't—couldn't—love him. Maybe once, she'd wanted him. And now, probably more than ever, she needed him. But that was all. He wouldn't settle for less than love. And she shouldn't settle, either.

He had to remind himself that Sarah was Seth's sister. Not his lover or woman or any other damn thing that was only going to beat up his heart even more if he couldn't shake these unrequited feelings for her.

But the feelings were there, and he couldn't completely ignore them. She *did* look tired. Hell, it was closer to 1:00 a.m. than midnight, and she probably thought she was going to school in the morning. Now was when he should offer to drive her home. There'd be another cop there. One at school, too. But she needed to understand that he'd be there somewhere, too. Supervising the others, shadowing their movements, keeping her safe.

"Seth asked me to take care of you," he announced without any fanfare. "Until he's up on his feet and can do it himself."

"Typical. Only twelve minutes older and he's got a big-brother complex that just won't quit." She tipped her chin, seeking something in his expression when she added, "What did you say?"

"I'm like that stray dog you just can't get rid of." But like her attempt at humor, the joke fell flat.

"Coop…"

"Hey, I'm here, aren't I?" He brushed a strand of hair off her cheek, looked down at the sexily crooked tilt of her lips. "This may be awkward as hell, but I'm here. I'll keep you safe."

Chapter Six

"I hear Seth Cartwright isn't dead."

Shaw McDonough picked up the broom he'd been pushing through the corridors of St. Luke's Hospital and carried it into the utility closet. He closed the door after him and pulled off the fake glasses that irritated the newly healed skin on the bridge of his nose. They were about as uncomfortable as the tinted contact lenses he wore, but they'd served their purpose well enough that he'd been able to sweep right past Cartwright's hospital room and the crowd of supporters waiting to hear an update on his condition from the doctors—without a single one of those clueless cops recognizing him.

But now wasn't the time to gloat at the success of his plan for retribution. Theodore Wolfe, Sr., sounded pissed. Shaw needed to concentrate to maintain control of this phone call. "Where did you hear that?"

"You're not the only man I pay good money to for information on our operation in the States. I just received the disturbing call. Interrupted tea and my read of the *London Times*." Theodore Wolfe paused, probably puffing on one of those big cigars that would soon become Shaw's own private stash when he took over the Wolfe organization. "I ordered you to hit them hard. Hit them now."

So who was ratting him out to the boss? Shaw looked around the closet, as though he'd find the traitor here with him. He didn't like competition for Mr. Wolfe's approval. "You don't want Cartwright to just die, do you? You want him to suffer first." *He* did.

"I'm not comfortable when you make such a game of things. That's when mistakes happen. Toy with them if you want—but I expect the job to be done. And soon. I want Seth Cartwright dead and his family grieving. If you can't do it, I'll find someone who can."

"I haven't failed you yet. Just let me do this in my own way. You won't be disappointed."

"I better not be. I would be most…unhappy…if I had to make a trip to the States myself."

Shaw straightened to attention for that one. He didn't need the old man coming here and taking charge of anything. He'd worked too hard to position himself as Wolfe's number-one man on this side of the pond to be pushed back down in the hierarchy now. The British accent he worked so hard to hide slipped into his voice. "The authorities issued you a new passport?"

"Please. Scotland Yard may have identified me as a person of interest in some illegal activities, but, like Interpol, they can't tie anything directly to me. Without evidence, they can't stop me from traveling. And since I have some legitimate investments in the U.S. uncon-nected to the ones KCPD seized from Teddy's estate, the authorities there can't stop me from entering the country, either." He sounded pleased that he could assert his power over the law-enforcement officials who had tried for decades to pin something on him.

He sounded like he was asserting his power over Shaw as well. Perhaps he'd made an error in judging when the old man would be ready to retire. Oh, how he hated fawning over the Wolfes. But it had to be done. "That's good news, of course, sir. But I doubt there will be a need for you to come here. I have the Cartwright situation under complete control."

"I hope so." For the moment, he sounded appeased. "By the way, my inside man faxed me some interesting information. When you took care of Dawn Kingsley for me, apparently there was a witness."

"What?" Shaw McDonough didn't make mistakes. He was the one who'd always cleaned up Teddy's mistakes. Like Dawn. The pregnant tramp who could have turned the black-sheep son into his father's golden boy. Now that bitch was still causing him trouble from beyond the grave? "I paid off the only witness. Your man, Longbow, who helped me move the body." Of course, Ace Longbow was in jail now, serving time for multiple domestic assaults and the attempted murder of his ex-wife. "Is Longbow talking?"

The big guy normally kept his mouth shut about company business. But if he thought exposing him for Dawn's murder would get him out of jail sooner and back on the trail of his ex, then…

"It's not Ace. It seems Teddy was entertaining female company the night you dealt with that gold digger. She was hiding in the suite somewhere and saw the whole thing. According to my KCPD contact, she described your old face to a *T.*"

He didn't even consider the fact that he'd altered his appearance so much that even the most reliable witness would have trouble identifying him. Someone was out there who could expose his true motivation for killing Dawn, someone whose testimony could ruin his perfect plan for stepping in as the heir to the Wolfe International empire.

And, of course, the traitorous informant was a woman. Just like Danielle.

Learning a witness's name meant Wolfe's inside contact had access to KCPD information. But identifying the rival was less important than identifying the woman who'd seen his face.

"Give me her name." He was already looking forward to killing her.

"If you like games, you'll love this one."

"Her name?"

"Sarah Cartwright."

SARAH WATCHED THE YOUNG OFFICER at the back of her classroom while he tried not to smile at the teacher's aide, who seemed quite smitten with his swarthy good looks. While Sarah continued to lead the students through the composition example she'd written on the overhead, Mickey Sandoval's eyes swept the room from side to side, taking note of the younger students on the playground outside the window as well as the custodian walking past Sarah's door in the hallway. If there was something amiss that could endanger Sarah, and thus, the school, Mickey would spot it.

Or so she hoped.

After shifting the discussion to word choice and giving the students their writing assignment, Sarah sank into the chair behind her desk and stifled a yawn. Man, she was exhausted. But she'd had trouble sleeping last night, keyed up with worry over Seth's injuries. She'd been wracking her brain over what the notes that she, her mother and Rebecca had received might mean. Then she'd spent several minutes hating her father even while she missed him.

And even longer wondering at the shameless way she'd turned to Cooper Bellamy for support and comfort last night. Again.

She had no right to demand anything from him, and yet…

She shivered inside her sweater as her body craved the warmth that Cooper's body had provided.

She got up and walked around the classroom, answering questions and making suggestions as the students rewrote the exercise she'd assigned. As she neared the back of the room, her gaze drifted to Mickey. He obviously made Miss Houdek's and even some of the ten-year-old girls' pulses race. He was effortlessly handsome. Funny. Polite.

But she didn't feel a twinge of anything beyond objective appreciation. Did the foreign looks and trace of an accent remind her too much of the stupid infatuation she'd had with Teddy Wolfe? Were her hormones so focused on the baby's needs that she couldn't feel attraction to any man?

Or had her idea of tall, dark and handsome shifted somewhere toward tall, blue-eyed and built to wrap around her just so? Despite the differences in their heights, she fit into the circle of Cooper Bellamy's arms the way a diamond solitaire fit into its setting. Aligned against his chest, tucked beneath his chin with his broad shoulders to lean into. His long arms could shield her and her baby from any trouble the outside world tried to throw at her.

Sarah shivered again, tingling with remembered warmth and gentleness, not cold. Trembling with a feminine desire fueled by raw masculine strength.

She could feel things, all right.

Wow. Sarah pushed her sleeves up to her elbows, feeling flushed with a sudden, embarrassing heat. She hurried back to her desk for a drink of water. Great. Just what she needed to be doing in the middle of her classroom, lusting after a man whom she'd hurt down to the bone. Coop was right to be cautious with his feelings around her. What if lust was all this was? What if security was all she craved?

Maybe she'd inherited her father's weak genes. Gambling was his weakness; making bad choices with men was hers.

Coop deserved someone wonderful and trustworthy. A woman who was sure of what she wanted—and that she wanted him. A woman who would be there for him when he needed her, just as he would surely always be there for the woman he loved.

Maybe Seth had been right all along in steering her

away from a relationship with his partner. But not for the reasons he preached. *She* wasn't good enough for Coop. Not the other way around.

The announcement bell rang over the intercom, thankfully interrupting her turbulent thoughts. A quick glance at the clock's odd time warned her this wasn't about tomorrow's lunch menu.

"Attention, students, faculty and staff. This is Dr. Pickering. We have a Code Black. Repeat, Code Black. Get your coats and file outside, following fire-drill procedures. Teachers, take your attendance books with you and verify each student's presence when you reach your assigned room at the church. I repeat. Code Black."

Sarah shivered. This time from outright fear.

Mickey Sandoval rose to his feet, his hand near the gun on his belt as he hurried to Sarah's side. "Is that what I think it is?" he whispered.

Sarah nodded. "Everyone get your coats and line up quickly at the door. Don't open any lockers along the way. Just go straight to the playground."

She helped one child with his jacket, steered another toward the door when she wanted to question what was going on. Mickey already had her coat in hand when Sarah grabbed her purse and the attendance book and led the way out the door. Students were pouring out of every room. Some of the youngest ones were crying. Chattering was shushed. Teachers were counting heads and some had already spotted the uniformed officer and his panting, muscular dog coming down the hall with Dr. Pickering.

Sarah kept moving. *My fault. My fault. This is all my fault.*

This was no drill. And despite the guilty panic screaming inside her head, Sarah marched her class outside to the playground and on to the nearby church a block away.

Code Black.

Bomb threat.

"DEREK. GET BACK HERE. We have to wait in the Sunday School room until your grandmother comes to pick you up." Sarah hugged her arm around Tammy's shoulders to bring her with her when she walked to the door to check the commotion from the hallway for herself.

"Dr. Pickering!" someone shouted.

"Where's my boy?"

"Daniel?"

"But Mrs. Obermiller said I could go."

"Would you mind answering a few questions?"

"Mark?"

"Alex?"

"Megan?"

"Tanya?"

Crazy, Sarah thought to herself, directing one fifth-grader back to his teacher and cringing at the television camera coming in through the double glass door of the vestibule. There was probably a 99.9 percent chance that she was responsible for all this craziness.

A phone call had come into her office, Dr. Pickering had said. *"There's a bomb in the school. Get out while you can. This is no joke."*

There was nothing that specifically mentioned Sarah's name or her brother's or mother's. Nothing about

Dawn Kingsley's murder or the investigation into Wolfe International. But after a stranger had come to the school… After Seth had nearly died yesterday… What other logical explanation could there be than that she was the target?

Justin Grant, leader of the TAC team—a KCPD technical assistance unit commonly referred to as the bomb squad— strode into the building, dodging the television camera and pulling Dr. Pickering aside. Hopefully, after more than an hour, he was reporting that the school was clear, that his search team of men and a dog had found no trace of any kind of explosive device, that the unidentified caller had been bluffing.

But why make such a call if there was no bomb? Sarah wasn't sure which alternative she found more disturbing—a man who'd frighten innocent children for no apparent reason, or a man who saw these kids as expendable collateral damage in whatever sick game he was playing with her.

"Miss Cartwright? I see my dad."

Sarah smiled down at Tammy's tearstained face. "You go on, then. You'll be all right. Try to have a good weekend."

Tammy rousted a smile in return, bringing color to her chubby cheeks. "You, too, Miss C. See ya."

After waving goodbye, Sarah pulled her attention back into the room to her remaining students. Officer Sandoval had struck up a conversation with her aide, Miss Houdek. *Hmm.* Maybe something good would come of this, after all. Like a hot date on Saturday night?

Maybe if she'd been more assertive about meeting

men herself, if she hadn't been quite so willing to rely on her father's matchmaking deals, she wouldn't be in this mess now. None of them would. Sarah shook her head and returned her focus to her students. "Crazy."

To the students' credit, *they* were following the rules, for the most part. It was the frightened parents and curious neighbors and persistent reporters arriving at the church who crowded into the church's parking lot and raised the energy level inside and around the church to a chaotic pitch.

When a familiar black pickup truck zipped into the circular drive outside the church's front door, Sarah exhaled a deep weight of tension she didn't realize she'd been holding.

Cooper Bellamy was here.

The school's uniformed officer ran up to have him move the vehicle, but Coop flashed his badge as he climbed out, said something that made the other policeman nod, point to the building and then back away to resume traffic control.

Sarah found herself gripping the frame of the door and leaning forward in anticipation as Coop's long strides quickly carried him inside the church. As soon as he swung open the big glass door, his gaze locked on to hers.

He hadn't done a thing yet but show up, and she already felt a shade more secure and calmer now that he was here. He stopped to talk to Justin Grant and her principal. But she'd already nodded that she was okay, hoping that's what those piercing blue eyes were asking of her.

"Miss Cartwright? Miss Cartwright!" Angelo Logan

came zooming down the hall, slightly breathless as he pushed his way through a crowd of children and parents.

"Whoa, there." She caught his shoulders, helping him stop before he crashed into her. "Good grief, Angelo. You know we don't run in the hallways, whether we're at school or here."

"He's here." The young man's shoulders rose and fell as he gulped in deep breaths. "Outside. I saw him."

Sarah's grip tightened. "The man who gave you the note?"

"Uh-huh." He pointed to the parking lot. He was backing up. Sarah followed. "I saw him with the people standing around on the sidewalk."

"You mean the spectators? The neighborhood people watching us?"

"Yeah. This way." He tugged on her hand and opened the glass doors.

Angelo's excitement over his discovery fueled Sarah's wary urgency. "Show me."

"Over—"

"Don't point." She snatched Angelo's wrist when he raised his arm to identify the man. She lowered her voice to a whisper, though the noise from the crowd would no doubt drown out her words. "I don't want you going anywhere near him. Just tell me what he looks like."

Sarah made a quick mental picture of Angelo's stranger, silently promising to reward the ten-year-old for his eye for detail. "Black hair, fishing hat, running suit," she repeated. She patted him on the back, then turned him away from the sidewalk to a waiting car. "Go find your mom. I'll take care of this. And thanks."

With Angelo bundled up safely with his mother, Sarah turned her attention to the group of people lining up between the parking lot and the street. A damp autumn wind blew her ponytail across her cheek. She brushed it back behind her collar and wished she'd thought to bring her jacket. There was a bite to the air that cut straight through to her skin. Though maybe the chill bumps had as much to do with the possibility of coming face-to-face with the man who'd dared to terrorize her family as much as they did with the temperature.

That one was too young. Wrong hair. No hat. Wrong clothes.

One man broke apart from the group and moved farther down the sidewalk as she approached. But he was only jockeying for a better position to view the proceedings from his side of the line the police had cordoned off.

Another man in the back moved. Black hair. Sarah straightened. *Damn.* If only she was a half foot taller. He disappeared behind a TV camera for a moment, then reappeared farther down the line. His hat wasn't exactly what she'd call a fishing cap—no hooks, no lures. But its tweed material had the same sort of floppy-brimmed—

A hand locked around her elbow and Sarah screamed.

"Hey, where are you going?" She glared into the eyes of Mickey Sandoval. "Are you trying to get me fired?"

"Let go of me." Frowning, she jerked free of his grip and spun back toward the spectators. She'd lost him. She circled the last row of cars in the parking lot and walked straight toward the sidewalk. Where was the hat? Brown tweed. Black hair. Sunglasses.

On this overcast day, the creep was wearing sunglasses. Had to be him.

"Miss Cartwright." Sandoval tugged at her sleeve. "You shouldn't be out here unescorted. Detective Bellamy already chewed me out for losing track of you."

There. Crossing the street. Climbing into a sleek black car.

"Hey!" Sarah spared Sandoval a glance over her shoulder. "That's the man who gave me that note. One of my students identified him." She pushed her way through the crowd. "We have to stop him."

"No. We don't have to—"

"Sarah?"

"Let go!"

The man tossed his hat into the seat beside him and started the engine.

"Stop him! He's getting away."

"Sarah!" It was a different voice calling to her, but she needed answers.

"Miss? What's going on? Did they find a bomb?" Someone jammed a microphone in her face. The crowd jostled her. Sandoval got pushed aside.

"You! Stop!"

The man peeled off his sunglasses and grabbed at his face. Something was wrong. His windows were up, but she knew cussing when she saw it.

Sarah broke free from the crowd, but a line of cars drove past, keeping her on the curb. She had to wait for the third one to drive by before she spotted him again. Whatever had bothered him had been dealt with. He shifted the car into gear.

"Sarah!"

The driver turned. Looked right at her.

Sarah froze.

The clothes were all wrong, the hair different. Even the shape of the nose and chin weren't familiar.

He smiled.

Sarah lurched on her feet as though she'd been struck.

The engine revved, tires burned the pavement and the car pulled into traffic and sped away.

But not before she'd gotten a glimpse of his eyes. One blue. One brown, nearly black. Cold, conscience-less black.

"Oh, my God."

"Sarah Elizabeth Cartwright!"

"Miss Cartwright."

She turned to Sandoval first. "Did you get the license? Did you see the license plate?"

"No, I was looking for you."

Sarah turned toward the other voice, chanting the facts before fear made her forget. "Black sedan. C-1-6, something-something-something. Black sedan… Coop?"

She spun around and ran smack into a tall, hard chest. She would have bounced off and fallen if Coop hadn't caught her by the arms. "Sarah. What the hell—?"

"I saw him."

He was already turning her into his arms, angling her away from the spectators and cars, forcing her into double-time to keep up with his long stride as he pushed through the crowd and led her back to his truck. "Saw who? What are you talking about? Why the hell would you run away from the man protecting you?"

"Coop. Stop!" She dug in her heels and yanked at his arm, forcing him to turn and face her. She snatched up handfuls of the front of his jacket and leaned in until she hit the solid wall of his chest. She tipped her head back and met his anger and frustration head-on. "You have to listen. I saw him. I saw Shaw McDonough.

"He's here in Kansas City."

Chapter Seven

"You're sure it was Shaw McDonough?"

Sarah gripped the door handle and hung on, rocking back and forth as Coop peeled around another corner and sped away from the traffic congesting the streets surrounding the school and church.

That was the fifth time he had asked her that question, and for the fifth time, with her stomach rolling, Sarah looked across the cab of his truck and answered, "Yes!"

But certainty was hard to hold on to when everything normal and reliable in her world was speeding away in the rearview mirror.

It had all happened so fast. If it *was* Shaw McDonough, he'd had some sort of plastic surgery to alter the shape of his face. He'd dyed his hair and let it grow down to his collar to make him look younger. He'd worn blue contacts, or at least one. That's probably what was giving him fits behind the wheel. His right contact was irritating his eye so he'd taken it out, or he'd lost it and was searching for it.

Identifying a man by the look in one eye was crazy.

But that was all she needed to see to feel that same horror. That same chill. That terrifying knowledge that the man did not give one damn about anyone in this world.

That ice-cold contempt had reached clear across the street and stabbed Sarah in the heart.

She'd had that feeling only once before in her life. Trapped in a closet, doomed to watch while a man blew a young woman's brains out and carted her off with the trash.

Sarah sank back into the velour upholstery, feeling suddenly, utterly exhausted. "Yeah. I'm sure it was him."

Her voice faded in volume, sounding weary and small, even to her own ears.

Coop finally slowed when he met with traffic, but his determination to reach whatever destination he had in mind never lessened. As they waited at a light, he reached across the seat and took hold of her shaking hand.

"Brrr." He turned his head and opened his mouth to speak but hesitated, as if he didn't trust himself to say anything more. The light changed and he turned his attention back to traffic. But he never let go.

Sarah didn't realize just how cold she was until she felt his warmth. She didn't realize just how exposed and vulnerable she felt until the strength of his big hand seeped into hers. Seizing the offered gift like a lifeline back to sanity, she turned her palm into his and held on with both hands.

Residential homes gave way to businesses. They traveled south toward I-70, pulled onto the interstate, then got off a few exits later.

"Where exactly are we going?"

"Away."

What kind of answer was that? "Could you be more specific?"

"I need some distance between you and him." The *him* he didn't have to explain. "I need time to think. Someplace where I don't have to watch your back for a few minutes."

"Shouldn't we be trying to track down the black sedan?"

"Oh, no—you are not going anywhere near that man again." For a split-second, Coop's grip pinched. Then he popped open his fist and pulled away, firmly wrapping both hands around the steering wheel. He apologized for the unfamiliar snap of his temper. "We're going to Blue Springs." A suburb. Okay, she understood that now. "The scenic route is to make sure no one's following us." Sarah glanced over her shoulder toward the stream of vehicles gathering for the rush-hour ride home. She hadn't even thought of that. "Don't worry," he reassured her. "They aren't."

She breathed a shade easier. "I don't see any big black cars."

"You shouldn't. Even with a partial plate number, we put out the APB soon enough that he should be contained to a relatively small area of the city. We'll find him."

But she heard the party line in his voice. "You hope."

"We hope." The blue eyes flickered her way. "McDonough was a clever enough bastard to slip through our fingers before. And if he's altered his appearance…"

"…We may never find him."

"KCPD may never find him," he corrected. "You have no business chasing after him the way you did this afternoon."

Was *that* why this typically good-natured man was so on edge? Did he think she'd cast away his concern—his promise to her brother—trying to be some kind of hero herself?

"I am not the naive, goody-two-shoes flower Seth thinks I am. Despite what you think, I was doing *my* job, protecting *my* class and *my* family. One of my students spotted him. How was I to know he wasn't in danger? Criminals don't like to be seen." She turned in her seat to face Coop as the scenery changed to rolling hills and matching suburban homes. "I wanted to identify the man who'd sent those threats. The kids' descriptions were all so varied that I know they weren't much use to your investigation. It was a way I could do something to help. How was I supposed to know it was…*him?*"

She crossed her arms at the unrelenting line of his jaw and with a huff of frustration faced the windshield again. He turned past a park dotted with lakes and autumn-colored trees and climbed a steep hill beside a rock fence, leaving the homes behind them and headed into the countryside.

"It doesn't matter what your reasons were, Sarah. One minute you're safely tucked away inside the church, and the next…" He tapped the wheel with a tight fist before drumming it against his thigh. "You made me crazy! You had no idea the bomb threat was a hoax yet, and then you go running off through the crowd where anyone could have abducted you or attacked you. Getting access to you through all that craziness to mask his intentions is probably why he called in the threat."

Sarah's own frustration lessened with the understanding of his. "But I'm okay."

"This is a man who likes to show that he's more clever than the rest of us. That he's controlling when and where he's going to hurt somebody." He tore his attention from the empty road and bathed her in the deep blue fire of his gaze. "Damn, Sarah, even if you're not worried about your own safety, you need to think of the baby."

"I said I'm okay. We're both okay."

Those blue eyes narrowed beneath a wry frown. "*I'm* not."

Without any more warning than that, he hit the brake and turned into a narrow gravel lane between two white rock markers. They skidded a bit as they climbed the hill toward a stand of evergreen trees surrounding a tall pole with the American flag flying on top.

Sarah looked around her. This was where Coop liked to think? "A cemetery?"

He turned onto a second, narrower lane. "It's peaceful. Quiet. From this vantage point you can see if anyone else pulls in. And my dad's here. It helps to think he's, you know, listening."

"Oh, Coop." Her heart squeezed in her chest at the bonds of love and family that ran so surprisingly deep within this man. "I…" *Don't know what to say.*

But he knew what to do. He slowed the truck and pulled off beneath an ancient pine. He ground the gears into Park, unhooked his seat belt and reached across the cab to undo hers. He was scooting toward her, lifting her, pulling. And she didn't resist.

"Sarah."

The raw gasp of her name spoke to something needy and feminine deep inside her. These last few days had been an emotional roller-coaster ride for him, too.

"Coop."

She climbed up onto her knees beside him to meet him halfway before he dragged her into his arms and crushed her against his chest. He tunneled his fingers into her hair, loosing her ponytail. He wound his arm so far around her back that he clasped her waist and squeezed his fingertips into her hip on the other side.

For a moment, Sarah was stunned by the unexpected ferocity of Coop's embrace. But as he rubbed his rougher cheek against hers and whispered husky endearments against her ear, she realized he simply wanted to hold her. He *needed* to hold her.

And she needed to be held.

"God, babe, I shouldn't let it get to me this much. I shouldn't care…" His hold tightened, pillowing her small breasts against his unyielding hardness. "But I do…care."

Sarah needed to feel him alive and warm against her, too. She wound her arms around his back and pulled herself immeasurably closer, burying her nose between his neck and collar, breathing in the scent of clean, musky heat that clung to his skin.

They held each other in silence like that for several minutes. Long enough for the tension to ease. Long enough for their breathing to synchronize so that each inhale created a warming friction, each exhale softened her against him. They held on to each other until the fears and frustrations abated and a new kind of awareness of each other's needs quietly took its place.

"Sarah?" He shifted his hand down to her buttock in a possessive grasp, then lifted and adjusted her onto his lap. "Not exactly the most romantic spot I could bring a girl, hmm?"

"Not exactly." She drew her hands down to a more neutral position, curling her fingers lightly into the soft nap of his denim shirt, turning her ear to the strong beat of his heart beneath it. "But I feel your strength—I feel calmer—here."

"Calm? Please tell me you're feeling some of this craziness, too."

She was tucked into that perfect cocoon between the dip of his chin and the curve of his shoulders. But the heat of his lap searing her bottom and the roaming touch of his fingers up and down her back—going up to her nape and down to the flare of her hip, up into her hair and farther down the length of her thigh—were stirring her pulse with evocative sensations that had nothing to do with reassurance or comfort.

She tilted her head back to see the drowsy desire of his gaze fixed on her mouth. "I feel it, too."

He bent his head and touched his lips to hers in a whisper of a caress. She flattened her palms against his chest and waited for his mouth to descend again. The second kiss was equally gentle, equally restrained.

Sarah leaned in, fascinated to watch the tip of his tongue dart out to moisten his lips before he kissed her again. He squeezed her bottom lip between his, but it was still just a taste. Still just a tease of what he could really do to her mouth.

"Coop." With a breathy plea, she chased his lips and caught a soft kiss of her own before he pulled beyond her reach.

He'd freed her ponytail from its band and had sifted her hair through his fingers, cradling a palmful where he cupped her neck. His other hand had found a home on her hip, and his fingers had slipped beneath the hem of her sweater, creating one thumbprint of heat where he touched her waist, skin to skin.

He dipped his chin and kissed her again with a slow, seductive claim. And though she parted her lips for him, he pulled away instead of slipping in.

The delicious frustration of it all settled in a puddle of heat that pooled between her thighs.

What was he waiting for?

She wasn't used to a man taking his time with her. Wasn't experienced enough to feel that she could take control of this closeness and turn it into whatever she wanted.

But she did understand being hurt, and knew that a little encouragement could go a long way toward healing that hurt. She knew that kind and gentle had their place, but so did other, stronger needs.

The muscles in Coop's chest contracted beneath her hands when he kissed her again, as though he was fighting something within himself, holding himself back.

Sarah smiled when he lingered against her mouth.

Sometimes, even a man liked to be asked.

She raised one finger to touch the firm arc of his lower lip. "I hope your dad doesn't mind me saying this, but you are one hell of a kisser, Detective."

The lip curved beneath her fingertip. "Is that right?"

Grasping the brim of his KCPD ball cap, Sarah flipped it up out of the way. Then, with a laugh, she removed it entirely and tossed it aside. She was already stretching up when she palmed the back of his beautifully shaped head. "Now do it like you mean it."

"If you insist."

"I—"

His mouth covered hers, opening her, claiming her. His tongue slipped inside to stroke hers, and Sarah felt the instant, answering fire all the way down to her toes. She rubbed her palms over the unique smoothness of his scalp and moaned into his mouth when the thumbprint at her back became a pair of hot, grasping hands beneath her sweater.

Coop's mouth angled this way and that, testing, tormenting, taking. His calloused caresses swept along her spine as his mouth moved against hers. His fingers slipped beneath the hook of her bra. Then one adventurous hand followed the crimp of elastic around to the front. At first he fingered her through the lace.

"Coop," she gasped.

"Yeah?" He flicked. She shuddered. "Like that?"

"You're ba...ad!" Sarah cried out as the extra-sensitive peak pearled beneath his branding palm and shot sparks of pure, perfect longing across every nerve and through every pore.

"And you're so good." Coop's lips grazed along her

jaw, nibbled on the lobe beside the earring she wore. "So sweet." He shifted the trunks of his thighs beneath hers, seeking a more comfortable position for the swelling desire that matched the intensity of her own, slow-burning arousal.

Talk about craziness! Sarah could barely think anymore. She was consumed with wanting, feeling, needing, reacting.

She'd felt ashamed, alone, frightened for so long.

But Coop made her feel connected, whole, smart again. "Your breasts are fuller than I remember. But so beautiful, so responsive to every touch."

Were there other parts of her he remembered? Other changes he had noticed? Things that reminded him of—

Coop's possessive fingers stopped at the unhooked button of her slacks. His palm rested over her belly, over the life inside her.

Over another man's baby and the cruel irony it represented.

Suddenly, Cooper's still hand felt cold against her. His hesitancy to continue the kiss kindled a regret that burned almost as hot as their passion had.

"I'm sorry," he began. "I wasn't even thinking about the baby. I didn't hurt you or him…her… Did I?"

"No. Of course, not." Sarah pulled her hands from inside his jacket and beneath his collar and curled them into her lap. "I'm the one who's sorry. We're a package deal and I forgot that for a moment. I forgot where we were. I was only thinking about…you. And what I wanted. I…" She pushed up onto her knees and moved away from the endearing awkwardness of his hands smoothing her clothes back into place. Coop's father should be proud of the strong, caring man his son had become. *She* was the one his dad probably wouldn't approve of. Sarah slinked over to her side of the truck cab, sidling up against the mind-clearing coolness of the window glass. "There are bigger things at stake here than what I want."

"Am I what you want?"

"Maybe. I mean, obviously, I want something from you. But how can I trust my judgment anymore? What if it's just the friendship and closeness I crave? That's hardly fair to you." She tugged at the lump she was sitting on and pulled out Coop's crumpled hat. She punched it back into shape and held it out like the inadequate peace offering it was. "And I'm pretty damn sure I'm not the woman you used to have a thing for. I've known for a long time that you liked…the old me." He snatched the cap from her fingers but toyed with it instead of putting it on. "But like I said, I'm a package deal now. With a mobster's baby growing inside me. I'll never be…I *can't* ever be that same Sarah Cartwright again."

"Wait a minute." His eyes narrowed as he turned his head her way. "What do you mean, a mobster's baby?"

Sarah shrank from the hollow sound of suspicion in his voice. Telling the truth about the life she carried would be the final brick in the wall of hurts and missteps that would keep her and Coop from coming together in any kind of real, lasting relationship.

But the truth was the only thing of value she could give him. "Teddy Wolfe is the only other man I've slept with since college. It was one horrible, humiliating time—and we used protection. But if the baby can't be yours, then…it must be his." She swallowed down a lump of shame and regret. "I was stupidly infatuated with him and I believed he was interested in me. I didn't understand what he really was before that. I knew within seconds after it happened that I'd made a terrible mistake. I was with him the night Dawn Kingsley was murdered. That's why I was there on the Riverboat to witness it. I was hiding from Teddy—and then Shaw McDonough came in with Dawn and… Say something."

"You slept with Teddy Wolfe. And the next day you slept with me?"

Tears burned behind Sarah's eyelids. "I was so hurt, so afraid that morning. I needed someone to care, someone I could trust. I needed…you."

Cooper's stony silence filled the air between them.

"I'm sorry." Understanding that some disappointments—some betrayals—couldn't be fixed with words, Sarah accepted the blame for hurting him. "So you see? I'm not the same woman I used to be." She summoned the courage to lift her eyes to meet Coop's unreadable gaze. "That boring, naive me was the woman you wanted. Not the tramp who can't tell a self-absorbed criminal from a real hero. I'll never be Seth Cartwright's innocent twin sister again. And she's the woman you had a crush on."

"You done talking?"

She tried to make sense of that disapproving scowl, and finally attributed his displeasure to a frustrated arousal, learning she carried the enemy's child and too much talking for any man.

Finally she nodded.

"Then stay put for a few minutes." He climbed out of the truck and strode over to the veterans' memorial, where he saluted the flag before circling it and kneeling in front of a single grave marker.

Sarah turned away, giving Coop his privacy to say whatever he had to say to his father's memory. She curled up in her seat to study the graying sky and fight off a little pang of envy that he shared more faith and trust and love with his father after his death than she shared with her own living excuse for a father. Why couldn't she have seen what kind of men the Bellamys were before she'd gotten that crazy notion to get involved with Teddy Wolfe? Why had she trusted her father with her love life when he'd shown her time and again that he couldn't be trusted for much of anything? Why had it taken her too long to grow the wisdom she needed to see that a better man—the best man—had been a part of her life all along? Now it might be too late to make even a friendship work with Coop.

So many mistakes. How could she ever get past them?

It wasn't so many minutes later that Coop returned. "You okay?"

Not really. But she'd get through this. "I will be. Are you okay?"

His lack of an answer was equally telling, although he seemed calmer, more focused—more distant—than he'd been a few minutes ago. This stern, introspective version of Coop felt like a stranger compared to the handsome man with the ready smile she'd known for so long.

The time it took him to put his hat back on was plenty of time to remember the boatload of guilt she carried.

And not just when it came to hurting Coop again. "Why was I even at school today? Why did I listen to Captain Kincaid and assume it was okay to go on with my life as though nothing has happened to me?" She automatically fastened her seat belt when Coop turned the truck around and drove north toward the city again. "I put every one of those children in danger."

"There was no way for McDonough to know you *wouldn't* be at school today. He might have called in that bomb threat whether you were there or not. And if he did somehow know you were AWOL, he could have threatened the school just to flush you out of hiding anyway."

"Great. So no matter what I do, I'm a risk to those kids."

The cell phone on Coop's belt rang. He checked the number before answering it. "Bellamy. What do you have, Sandoval?"

He listened as he drove, not liking what he was hearing if the muscle twitching in the tight clench of his jaw was any indication. He glanced once at Sarah, while still speaking into the phone. "No mistake. It *was* McDonough. Theodore Wolfe's enforcer."

Sarah nodded and he turned his attention back to the road ahead of them. She dug her fingers into the arm-rest when he swore. "What is it?" she asked, already fearing the answer.

"Run the name," he told Sandoval. "We can expand the search area as soon as we get an updated composite to put out on the wire." He paused. "Yes, call Kincaid and fill him in. Better yet, I'll do it. You just run the name for me."

Coop ended the call, then just as quickly, rested the phone on the dashboard to scroll through and find another number. She was getting a glimpse of the old Coop again. Cooper Bellamy, the cop. Determined. Thorough, with impeccable timing. The man who carried a gun. The man who'd stood between her and her father more than once. The man her brother trusted with his life. And now with hers.

This man was all business. Not the lanky sidekick who'd always made her laugh. Not the tender protector who could kiss her until she forgot everything but him.

Detective Bellamy scared her a little.

"What is it?" she asked.

"A black-and-white patrol found the car from the description you gave us. A black Lexus, rented to an Ian Smythe. It was abandoned, with no sign of McDonough."

"*Ian Smythe?* An Anglicized John Smith? That's pretty lame for an alias. Wouldn't anyone with half a brain at the rental company question… Wait a minute. Don't you have to have a credit card and a driver's license to rent a car?"

Coop nodded. "Yeah. That means our man has false papers and accounts he can access for money. Probably under more than one identity. That means McDonough could be hiding right under our noses anywhere in the Kansas City area, and he'd be almost impossible to find."

Sarah sank back into her seat, her left hand moving to shield her belly, even though she wasn't sure yet if she loved or hated the child growing inside. Shaw McDonough…? Ian Smythe…? He could be anybody on the streets, in one of the cars Coop was passing now, perhaps. He could be anywhere—the school, the hospital, the grocery store—and she'd never even know it. Not until it was too late. Not until she was dead.

"He saw my face," she murmured, remembering that coal-black eye, remembering that smile.

"What's that?" Coop asked.

Taking a deep breath, Sarah steeled her voice. "McDonough. This afternoon. The way he smiled at me. He knew who I was. He knows I'm the woman who could testify against him."

"KCPD never released your name as the witness who saw Dawn Kingsley's murder. If McDonough seemed to recognize you, it's because you're Seth's sister, or a crusading teacher who messed up his plans today. Not because you saw him pull a trigger."

But Sarah wasn't so sure. Any police department, whether intentionally or not, could leak information to the press or to public or private individuals. It all depended on finding the right person with the right motive at the right price.

Maybe Coop wasn't so sure, either. He selected a number and put the phone back to his ear.

"Who are you calling now?"

"John Kincaid. I'm taking you to a safe house."

COOP'S EYES FELT AS IF THEY HAD enough grit in them to make him think he was crawling through a sandstorm instead of dragging through his forty-eighth hour with nothing more than a couple of short naps to sustain him.

Still, his ears were attuned to the rundown of security protocols Atticus Kincaid—the "smart one" of John

Kincaid's four sons, according to the task force captain—
and his team had put into place. Thick brick exterior,
bulletproof glass and steel doors on the unassuming
house. Remote yet accessible location in a less-popu-
lated corner of north Kansas City. Two men in the house
at all times, two uniformed officers providing routine
drive-bys and surveillance of the area outside. All of them
trained in hostage-protection strategies. Hourly check-ins
with Task Force Commander John Kincaid. Flak vests,
locks, codes, alarms—and an automatic escape procedure
in place should McDonough, Wolfe International or
anyone else breach the system and get too close to Sarah.

Atticus pulled off his reading glasses and tossed them
on top of the neighborhood map he'd unfolded over the
coffee table. "Make sense?"

Coop nodded. "Sounds pretty thorough to me. I appreciate the information, even though I'm not officially
on your team."

"You're part of the task force, so no problem." Atticus
stood when Coop did. "I know the loose ends of this
Wolfe investigation have been keeping Dad up at night.
So if this is how I can help, I'll do it. You know, Dad
should be slowing down these days, thinking about retirement. Instead, he's trying to track down a murderer
we can't even ID and get his hands around Theodore
Wolfe's throat. Talk about an untouchable."

"I thought Captain K was up for the deputy commissioner position."

"He is." Atticus gestured to the main hallway and
followed Coop toward the driveway-side door. "To him,

a desk job like that *would* be retirement. He wouldn't mind slowing down for Mom's sake, but as long as he has unfinished business with Wolfe or anyone else, Dad won't take the job."

Coop grabbed his jacket off the coat tree and slid into the khaki camo sleeves. He pulled his ball cap out of his pocket and plumped it back into shape. "That's a shame. Your dad has the reputation that could bring back the respect the position deserves."

Shrugging at the praise for his old man, Atticus combed his fingers through his wavy black hair, which he shook loose over his collar. "Yeah. He does. Thanks."

With a nod, Coop headed past the bathroom where he knew Sarah was changing and getting ready to catch at least a few hours of sleep. It was probably best to leave without saying goodbye. To leave before he saw her again and was tempted to stay. Even the news that the baby she was carrying belonged to Teddy Wolfe didn't stop him from wanting to protect her. But Atticus Kincaid was a good cop. He'd keep Sarah safe. He was more specifically trained for protection work than an investigator like Coop was, and better rested, besides. Plus, he wouldn't be distracted by twisted-up feelings and a relentless attraction to the woman.

He damn well better not be.

That flare of some territorial claim on Sarah was reminder enough that he needed to leave and let Atticus do his job. He was still keeping his promise to Seth to watch over his sister, but he was being smart about it by setting her up here in the midst of far more security than he could provide on his own.

The two men entered the kitchen to find Mickey Sandoval working at the counter and chattering away on his cell phone. "I don't know what she thought she saw. I was looking at the same crowd of people. I didn't see anybody matching the description. Stocky Brit. Forties. Short, peppery hair. Yeah, dude. I think she had a panic attack and just imagined he was the cause of it. I mean I can't blame her after what happened to her brother. But, *dios,* McDonough's thousands of miles away, right? We don't have to—"

"You can shut up anytime now."

Startled by the low-pitched threat, Sandoval almost dropped his phone. He turned and tried to stare down Coop. "Hey, this is a private conversation."

"Your point?" Was there any good excuse for bad-mouthing Sarah's competency and making light of her fears?

Mickey might be young, but he wasn't stupid. He finally got the look. "Right. I'm shutting up now. Sorry." He pulled the phone back to his ear. "I'll talk to you later, dude." He hung up, wasted his time apologizing again, then wisely changed topics. "You were right, Kincaid—this kitchen is stocked." He wrapped something up in a tortilla and scooted past Coop and Atticus. "I'll just, uh, check the front of the house."

"Good plan." Coop slipped his cap on and tugged down the brim. "You won't mind if I check in on you tomorrow?"

"You mean check to see if Sandoval's screwed up anything else yet?" Atticus *was* the smart one. "Just make sure you call first. I don't like surprises."

Coop grinned. "I don't blame you."

He heard soft, quick footsteps in the hall, and, a moment later, his favorite frustrating blonde appeared in the open doorway. "Wait a minute. You're not staying?"

Oh, boy. Coop's lungs emptied on a weary sigh. How was he supposed to walk away from the plea in those pretty green eyes?

He tried a joke. "I've been up for most of two days. I need my beauty sleep."

In answer, she hurried across the kitchen in her bare feet and a pair of men's flannel pajamas that would have been big even on him. With the pant legs rolled up to her ankles and the sash from a plaid robe cinching it all together at her waist, she made a comical picture.

But the joke was on him.

She walked right into his chest, circled her arms around his waist and hugged him tightly. "Don't go."

"Sarah—"

"Please. I know I hurt you." She snuggled closer, and Coop squeezed his eyes shut against the instantaneous fire that bloomed across his skin. "But this is where I feel safest."

Ah, hell. His arms were around her and his lips were in her freshly washed hair long before he became aware of the twin thrust of her breasts poking against his stomach, and that firming, rounding, most vulnerable part of her pressing even lower against him. She was all delicate, all female, and—for this moment, at least—all his. "I've gotcha, babe. I've gotcha."

"I'm scared to death, Coop," she whispered against his shirt. Her lips teased the muscles beneath like a caress, and he shuddered. "Not just for me. For Seth. My family. The school. Anyone who gets in Shaw McDonough's way." Her fingertips lined up along his spine and pressed in. He adjusted his stance, moving one of his big feet between hers so they could stand as close as she wanted. "I don't feel like I'm in control of anything anymore."

"Neither do I," he admitted, dipping his nose in the fragrant dampness at her temple. "But I need you to be safe. And this is the best facility, these are the best men—"

"*You're* the best man I've ever known."

She lifted her head, leaning back against the brace of his hands, letting him look down and read the sincerity in her eyes.

"I have made some colossally stupid mistakes these past few months—trying to meet men who could… change my life, maybe help me get away from my dad's influence. I was trying to be someone I'm not, someone I don't want to be. I hurt people—I hurt you—in the process. And now I'm responsible for another little life who may pay the price for my misguided…rebellion." She sucked in a steadying breath before raising one hand to reverently touch his lips. "But one mistake I *never* made was knowing I could count on you."

It wasn't a declaration of love, but the idea that she understood what *should* have been there between them went a long way toward soothing his fractured pride and the sting of betrayal.

While she held on to him, Coop released her to brush his knuckles over the apples of her cheeks, to trail his fingertips along the fine line of her jaw and slip beneath the heavy weight of her hair. With the pads of his thumbs he traced the decadent fullness of her lower lip.

All the while he was lowering his head, studying every nuance of her reactions to his touch, moving closer, ever closer. "I will always be there for you, Sarah. Always."

He whispered the vow against her lips before covering them with his own.

His kiss was slow, deliberate, and the depth of her response was a humbling, arousing, all-consuming thing. Every time he kissed her it was like this—like a truth, a power, a promise linking them together.

But, like every other kiss, his timing left a lot to be desired. There was work to be done, sleep to be had— priorities and brothers and bad guys to be dealt with. And oh, yeah, wasn't there still an audience in the house?

Coop was smiling when he pulled away. Sarah's cheeks were flushed with healthy color, and her lips were slightly swollen with the stamp of his possession. From her needy, guileless, eager response, he knew damn well that Teddy Wolfe had never kissed her like that. No other man had. And he was okay with that.

He chuckled in the back of his throat at just how okay he was with that.

"Coop? What's so funny?"

He shrugged, knowing he'd better not answer that one. "Nothing. I should be going."

"Do you have to?"

"I'll be back tomorrow. I promise. But I have some thinking to do. And I have some sleeping that needs to happen. I won't be able to do either with you around to

worry about." He looked down at the pattern of pheas-
ants and deer dotting her voluminous pajamas and had
to make a joke. "I wouldn't be able to get anything done
with you runnin' around in this damn sexy outfit to
distract me, either."

Thankfully, she laughed, too. "It was either this or
Victoria's Secret. But I know what you like."

He planted a perfunctory kiss on her mouth and
pushed her away. "You get to bed. Exhaustion won't do
any of us any good. Remember, you're sleeping for
two." Without considering the impulse, he kissed the
tips of his fingers, then touched them to Sarah's stomach. "Good night, little one. See you tomorrow."

Sarah started at the gesture, then hugged her arms
across her stomach and backed away. But he could see
by the curious frown on her face that touching the baby
wasn't what had startled her, but that *his* willingness to
touch her there had. "We'll be here," she whispered.

"I'll hold you to that."

Sometime along the way, Atticus had discreetly
excused himself. But now, as Coop turned for the door,
he reappeared to say good-night and lock up behind him.

The spit of cold rain on his face revived Coop enough
to climb into his truck and drive himself home. Although
he doubted there was anything Mother Nature could do
to erase the lingering contentment Sarah's words and
kisses had created.

Though he could have driven the streets till dawn
trying to figure the best way to salvage a lasting relationship with Sarah Cartwright, Coop settled for calling
tonight a fair start among the series of events that always

seemed to drive them apart. Tonight's reluctance to let him go might have only been about fear, but he didn't think so. Her confession about mistakes and rebelling and Teddy Wolfe told him a lot about her wariness to get involved with him.

He wasn't naive enough to think that one kiss at the end of a very long, turbulent day meant there was smooth sailing ahead for them. When they caught Shaw McDonough—and he refused to think in terms of *if*—there would be a trial, and testifying wouldn't be easy for Sarah, not with the killer sitting there, staring her in the face while she was on the stand. She'd need time with her baby, to develop that bond she seemed almost afraid to latch on to because of the baby's father. Then there was Seth, and concerns about how a relationship with his sister would affect their friendship and partnership at work.

And, of course, there were those pesky little Coopers— or lack thereof. Could Sarah be content to pledge a lifetime to a man who couldn't give her children? Maybe it was worth a call to his urologist and oncologist to double-check just how slim those statistics about making babies were, or whether there were any new treatments or therapies to try.

And there was Sarah herself. She'd learned to *count* on him, she'd said. Security and reliability were probably pretty potent attractors for her right now. But could she learn to *love* him?

If she couldn't, would he be able to know the difference between gratitude and love? And would he be able to live with the answer, either way?

"Okeydokey," he said to the windshield wipers as the

sprinkles turned to a steady rain. "That's enough heavy thinking for one day."

The sky was black with clouds, and the rain obscured the streetlamps and headlights as he drove back to his apartment. It was well past visiting hours, but he stopped in at St. Luke's to check on his sleeping partner and trade hugs and updates with Seth's mom and Rebecca. Though it wouldn't have changed his mind on the best course of action for Sarah's safety, they both agreed that secluding her in a secure house with round-the-clock guards was the best plan. Commissioner Cartwright thoroughly approved of Atticus Kincaid's capabilities and promised that whatever Sarah needed would be provided. She left the room to call Sarah and make plans for visiting her tomorrow, taking Sarah some of her own clothes.

And although the commissioner raised an eyebrow when Coop suggested her daughter would need pajamas as well, she kissed his cheek and thanked him again for helping her. When he would have left, Shauna Cartwright-Masterson caught him by the arm and pulled him back to hug him tightly.

"Screw protocol," she said, holding on even when Eli crossed his arms and looked at Coop like he wondered what he was thinking, hugging his wife. She pulled away and turned right into the protective drape of her husband's arm across her shoulders. "Knowing my children are in danger is a hard thing for a mother to bear. I know they're grown-ups now, but…"

Eli kissed her temple. "We've gotten through scares like this before, boss lady. We'll get through it this time, too."

Shauna sniffed back a tear and nodded. "I'm counting on you, Detective."

"Yes, ma'am," Coop answered. Like mother, like daughter.

Feeling the extra burden of that praise and responsibility, Coop finally dragged himself home.

He ate two ham sandwiches, downed a quart of milk and then hit the shower. The shave could wait until tomorrow morning; he needed some shuteye.

An hour later he was wide awake, staring at the bedroom ceiling and listening to the rain fall outside his window. He hoped Sarah was tucked in beneath the covers, sound asleep while the thunder and lightning beat their way across the landscape. He didn't think that Sarah was afraid of storms, but a night this black gave way to other dangers. Flash floods. Power outages.

Shadows where men with evil intentions could hide.

Forty-five minutes later, Coop was parked in one of those shadows down the street from the safe house.

If Shaw McDonough wanted to get to Sarah, it wouldn't be tonight.

Chapter Eight

Sarah swallowed her last bite of wheat toast before carrying her plate and utensils to the sink and dunking them into the hot soapy water she'd started before breakfast. She had the dishes clean and in the drainer beside the skillet she'd washed earlier when Atticus Kincaid strolled into the room.

"I thought I smelled something good in here." His hair was still damp from his shower as he buttoned his cuffs and adjusted the sleeves. "You do know you don't have to cook for us, right?"

Nonetheless, he sat at the table across from Mickey Sandoval and picked up a spoon to serve himself the last of the scrambled eggs she'd prepared. Smiling as she dried her hands on the apron she wore, Sarah retrieved the serving bowl and spoon to wash them as well. "Trust me. I have to eat breakfast early every day or I get morning…" She caught herself just in time and covered the awkward pause by shoving the oversize pajama sleeves up past her elbows and dipping her hands back into the suds. "I get sick if I don't eat. It's probably a low-blood-sugar thing. And believe me, it's as easy to cook for three as it is for one."

"Well, thank you."

"No problem. Besides, it gives me something to do. Saturday morning cartoons just aren't what they used to be."

"If you say so."

"*Delicioso,* Sarah." Mickey's compliment was just as fervent as he polished off his plate and carried it to the sink for her to wash. He nodded toward the coffeemaker on the counter. "The coffee I fixed is ready. May I pour you a cup?"

She closed her eyes and inhaled deeply, savoring the deep, pungent aroma that filled the kitchen. "Mmm. *Delicioso,* yourself, Mickey. Smells fabulous." Yet she had to twist her face into a wry smile when she looked at him. "But I'm going to have to pass. My doctor said I shouldn't have any caffeine. That's why I didn't get it started myself. Thanks, anyway."

Atticus tapped his mug on top of the table. "Hey, I'll take you up on the offer."

"Yes, sir." Sandoval, looking somewhat crestfallen, set the mug he'd poured for her at his own place setting. Then he picked up a fresh mug and poured Detective Kincaid a cup of the steaming brew.

"Good stuff." Atticus's compliment seemed to renew Sandoval's smile. He was such a kid in a grown man's body, Sarah thought. So eager to please. "You brewed this yourself?"

Mickey was his old self already. "I can't take too much credit. The coffee beans were with the groceries the supply team dropped off for us last night. All I did was open a bag."

Sarah finished the rest of the dishes while the men drank their coffee and chatted about check-in schedules and duty assignments. They paused and thanked her again when she took off her apron and excused herself to go get dressed.

Her stomach heaved a little when she closed the door to the bathroom. "Power of suggestion," she said, glaring at the toilet. She pressed her hand to her stomach and concentrated on her reflection in the mirror over the sink, congratulating herself when mind won out over matter and her insides returned to normal. "Good job, Cartwright."

Lord, she looked like a ghost with the shadows under her eyes on her pale skin. But considering everything, she actually felt a little better this morning than she'd felt for a long time. Could be the solid seven hours of sleep she'd gotten—rainstorms always seemed to have that effect on her. Or the complete breakfast that filled her stomach and was staying with her. Or she could attribute this forgotten serenity and tinge of anticipation to the fact she'd finally realized some things last night, and, more important, she'd finally shared some of those truths and troubles with Coop.

She didn't feel like she was taking advantage of his feelings for her quite so much. She didn't feel like there was such a big wall of caution between them anymore. Oh, yeah, and wherever the man had learned to kiss like that, his teacher should be applauded.

Okay, remembering *those* few minutes in the kitchen last night brought some color into her cheeks.

She tried to remember back to the few minutes she'd spent with Teddy Wolfe. She'd been such an idiot to think he was the kind of man she wanted. Had he even kissed her? Funny how the memory of that particular nightmare seemed to fade into more pleasurable thoughts of Cooper Bellamy—holding her, kissing her, loving her.

"Okay, girl." When her cheeks turned crimson, she pushed even those thoughts aside and turned on the water in the sink. "One step at a time. We've got a long way to go yet." But he'd promised to come see her today. That deserved at least the hint of a smile.

Since she'd showered the night before, this morning Sarah simply washed her face and brushed her teeth. She was combing her hair when she heard someone out in the hall.

"Sarah?" She barely recognized the hoarse voice. Was that Atticus?

She jumped at the sound of something falling against the bathroom door. *"Occupado."* Like he didn't know? Maybe he wasn't feeling well. "Is everything okay?"

The doorknob rattled. "Open the door!"

Oh, my God. Something was wrong. Very wrong.

"Sarah?" He pounded on the door. "I need in there. Now!"

With alarm tensing every muscle, she unlocked and opened the door. "Are you feeling all—"

Atticus, acting drunk, stumbled in, clutching at her shoulders, his weight nearly dragging her to the floor.

"What the—?" She braced herself and sort of caught him, but mostly she got him turned so that he was collapsing onto the lid of the toilet. "Are you ill?"

He pushed a cell phone into her hand. "Call for help."

His words were slurred, his eyes rolling, and his glasses were nowhere to be seen.

"Atticus, what's wrong?" She pushed him against the back of the toilet and knelt beside him to prop him upright.

He was fighting to stay awake, to stay conscious. "Been drugged. Sandoval out. Can't see numbers. Call."

"Okay."

She opened the phone. But as soon as her hands left his chest, he collapsed, crumpling forward. Sarah dropped the phone and moved to try to break his fall. But the best she could do was keep his head from hitting the side of the bathtub.

He'd passed out!

What the hell was going on? "Atticus?"

She should check Sandoval, see if he was sprawled across the floor in the kitchen, make sure he was breathing.

But when she turned on the balls of her feet and tried to stand, Atticus's hand shot out and grabbed her wrist.

"A-a-ah!"

Sarah fell back to his side. He was unlocking his holster. "Can you use…a gun?"

"I know how." Her hands weren't much steadier than his as she helped him pull the heavy Glock from his belt. Oh, man, she hated this. "Why am I going to need a gun?"

He pushed the butt of the gun into her palm and pointed the barrel toward the hallway.

"Lock…door," were his last words before his grip went slack and his eyes rolled shut.

"Atticus!" She shook his shoulder. No response. She

pressed her fingers to his neck and thankfully found a pulse. But even a light smack at his cheek couldn't make his eyes open again. "Oh, my God." She was on her feet. "Oh, my God."

Sarah jumped over his legs to close and lock the bathroom door. Then she dove to the floor and dug the cell phone from beneath Kincaid's body.

She opened the phone and dialed.

"RIGHT, WALT." FUNNY HOW COOPER shared the same sarcastic tone as his uncle. "Like I'd tell you if it was girl trouble. I say I can't commit to Thanksgiving at your place because I might be busy, and you automatically assume it has something to do with a woman. I have a job, remember? Odd hours? Crime never takes a holiday and all that?"

He'd be damned if he'd mention how accurate Walt was in his assessment of what was occupying his mind this morning. The house he'd been watching in the next block was still quiet. Only a couple of the lights behind the shades had been turned on. After the stresses of yesterday and the late hour before she'd gone to bed, Sarah was probably sleeping in. He'd give her some time to wake up and maybe change before he knocked on the door and invited himself in for breakfast.

Uncle Walt laughed. Coop knew he was one person he could call early on a Saturday morning who wouldn't be just getting out of bed and who'd be glad to hear from him. After visiting his father's grave site yesterday, he'd been doing a lot of thinking about family. Talking with his uncle reminded him of that connection. Plus, it would divert enough time before he got too antsy to wait another minute to drive up to the safe house.

As he suspected, he'd caught his uncle out in his workshop. "Well, you know, Coop, I haven't stayed a bachelor all these years because I was gay or I couldn't find a woman. Your father and I had some mighty fine adventures before he met your mother. I could give you some pointers."

"So you keep telling me." Last night's storm had cleared away the clouds and filled the air with the earthy smell of wet leaves and grass. A black-and-white patrol unit rolled by on one of its routine sweeps, and Coop watched it turn the corner just beyond the house. Atticus had told him he wanted to keep the driveway free in case there was an emergency and vehicles needed to get in or out. "So, where are all these mystery women that you've loved and left along the way?"

"Don't pooh-pooh things you don't know about, son. You know I travel a lot."

"To teach seminars and do research."

"Partly."

It was Coop's turn to laugh. "So, Dad may have been the Marine, but you're the guy with a girl in every port?"

"Well, not *every* port."

Coop shook his head and grinned. He hadn't inherited his ability to flirt from his own dad, but the smart talk was obviously in the gene pool.

"You're sure I can't get you to change your mind about Thanksgiving?" Walt asked. "While you're here in St. Louis, I wanted to drive down and show you the lake cabin. I've been working on it all summer. The caretaker, Kenny Sterling, keeps everything running year-round. I've added lots of modern amenities so your mom won't feel like she's roughing it quite so much. You're welcome to bring a guest if you'd like."

Right. Like that ploy was going to get information about Sarah out of him. "We'll see. I just wanted to give you a heads-up so you wouldn't build on a spare room or something like that for me."

"A spare room, hmm?" Now the old man was thinking, planning, probably already sketching something out on the paper he kept in his workshop. "There's a lot of limestone in the ground behind the cabin. I could…"

Coop missed the rest of Walt's words when his phone beeped with an incoming call. "Hold on a sec, Walt. This may be work."

He checked the new call, read the name on the screen and frowned.

Pushing the talk button, he looked down the road at the quiet exterior of the brown brick house. But things were suddenly far from quiet inside him.

"Atticus?"

"It's Sarah. We need help."

SARAH HELD THE GUN BETWEEN both hands, her arms outstretched, and pointed it toward the door.

Why was this taking so long? Where was the help she'd called for? 9-1-1? Coop?

Okay, so she'd really only had time to fold up a towel and stick it beneath Atticus's head since that last call. But where were they?

The house was so deadly quiet. Was it safe to go out

and see if Sandoval was all right? Would she eventually pass out, too? It sickened her to think that she might have unknowingly ingested something that could harm the baby. But Mickey and Atticus had eaten the same things she had for breakfast. The only difference was that she'd drunk milk while they'd had... "The coffee."

Someone had drugged—poisoned?—the coffee. When? Where had it come from? The gun grew heavy in her hands as Sarah tried to think.

Mickey had opened the pouch of ground beans fresh this morning. Was the drug in there? Had something been added to the filter? The mugs? He said the supply unit had delivered the groceries last night. Had one of those officers doctored the coffee? Had someone else? Oh, my God, had Mickey?

Maybe Detective Sandoval had only pretended to pass out. Maybe he'd unlocked the door for an accomplice. Maybe he was standing right outside this bathroom right now!

"Don't do this, Cartwright," she warned herself, needing to hear a voice—anything—to keep her mind from wandering to frightening, traitorous thoughts. "Just hold the gun. Wait. Help will come." She swallowed hard and said what she was really thinking. "Come on, Coop. Don't let your timing be off now."

She screamed at the knock on the door and nearly tripped over Atticus's legs as she automatically backed away from the sound. *Real smooth, girl.*

"Miss Cartwright?"

Not Coop. *Don't be disappointed. Don't panic.* She steadied the gun and braced her feet on the cold tile floor, wishing she was wearing body armor instead of men's pajamas.

The man knocked again. "Miss Cartwright, are you in there? I'm Officer Burkhardt. I've been doing the drive-bys. When Detective Sandoval missed his check-in call, I thought I'd better stop by and see if everything was okay."

Just because she didn't recognize the voice didn't mean he wasn't telling her the truth.

"Ma'am?" He sounded courteous enough. Concerned enough. "I'm pretty sure things aren't okay. I found Sandoval passed out in the kitchen, and there's no sign of his partner. Miss Cartwright?"

This wasn't right. Something about this wasn't right.

But what was she supposed to do? Wait until the man broke down the door or shot his way in? What would her mother do? What would Seth do?

Where the hell was Coop?

"I'm in here, Officer." What a wimpy sound. She cleared her throat, steeled her nerves, steadied the gun and spoke again. "I'm in here. Detective Kincaid is here as well. He's been drugged, too."

"Are you hurt?"

If scared to death qualified as an injury, then yes. "No. I'm fine." But she still wasn't just going to open the door to a man she didn't know. "Give me your badge number. What precinct are you with?"

She could call her mother. Surely, if the commissioner made the request, that information could be verified in an instant. But the phone was in her breast pocket that drooped to her waist. She couldn't aim Kincaid's gun with one hand *and* make the call. "Hell."

Lowering the gun, she pulled out the cell phone and dialed the number. "I'm waiting, Burkhardt. What's your badge number?"

"Miss Cartwright, I'm on the phone now with back-up. Standard procedure is to remove you to a new location once a safe house has been compromised."

"Your badge number, Burkhardt!"

"2-0-3-2."

She managed a normal breath. "And your precinct?"

"Please, Miss Cartwright. Open the door."

"Your precinct!"

"North-central. Substation 23."

Her mother's phone went straight to voice mail. *Damn.* Sarah disconnected and dropped the phone back into her pocket. Steadying the Glock between both hands, she moved toward the door. "All right. I'm coming out. Back away from the door."

"That's good." He sounded relieved. Probably glad the commissioner's daughter hadn't reported him. "I'm backing away." His voice did sound more distant. "I'm right by the kitchen door."

Sarah unhooked the lock, then quickly pulled the door open and steadied the Glock with both hands again. She spared a glance toward the front door in case he had lied about his position, then stepped out of the john and swung around toward the kitchen.

"Whoa. Steady there." The stocky police officer, about six feet tall, held both hands up in the air as Sarah sought out his badge and name tag. *Burkhardt. 2032.* Everything about his uniform, from his dark blue cap to his steel-toed shoes, from his black gloves to his aviator glasses looked legit. "You're all right, Miss Cartwright. My car is parked right outside. We'll go out the back and I'll drive you straight to the new location."

"I want to wait to make sure Kincaid and Sandoval are okay. I called 9-1-1. They'll send an ambulance as well as police backup."

"But you're our main concern. Sandoval and his partner wouldn't want you to risk your life for them. And every minute you're not secured is a minute that McDonough fellow has to..."

Sandoval and his partner. He'd said that before. Atticus was Mickey's superior officer. They weren't partners. But maybe that was an assumption by a cop who didn't know them well. But a good cop wouldn't assume. What else had he said that didn't make sense?

"When Detective Sandoval missed his check-in call..."

It wasn't Mickey's job to call in.

"Miss Cartwright—"

"Take off your glasses." Sarah's heart was in her stomach. Her legs felt like lead as she started to back away. Oh. My. God. "Take off your glasses!"

The bastard smiled.

"You son of a bitch." She glanced toward the john. "You did this to them?"

"Technically, Sandoval did. You know, he's much too eager for people to like him. Last night, when I suggested that this new blend of coffee would please you and his partner, he was more than willing to serve it at breakfast this morning." Shaw McDonough peeled off his glasses and tucked them into his chest pocket. Her legs found the strength to retreat when he stepped toward her. "Unfortunately, it seems he forgot to pour you a cup. This would have been so much easier if you were unconscious."

Sarah stared down the barrel of her gun at the blue contact lenses. "I called for backup. They're on their way."

He kept advancing. "No, they're not. I canceled the request. Said it was a false alarm. Officer Burkhardt gave me the code word to confirm it before he died."

He'd murdered someone else? He'd killed a cop? *No one was coming to help her?* "Stay back."

"I don't think so." Her back hit the front door and he kept coming. "I don't like loose ends. I don't like witnesses when I'm working. And I don't like deviating from my plans. Conscious or not, you and I are driving away to a secluded location where I'll allow you to call your brother just before I kill you. My employer feels betrayed by Seth and would like him to suffer as much as possible." A trace of his British accent had slipped back into his voice, reminding Sarah of that awful night in Teddy's suite, and the awful things he'd said to Dawn Kingsley before and after her death. "Personally, I just want you dead. But orders are orders."

"You tried to kill my brother?"

The question seemed to irritate him. "No. I *succeeded* in injuring your brother. When I want him dead, he will be."

"I'm not going anywhere with you."

"You'll have to shoot me to stop me."

Sarah pulled the trigger. Twice.

McDonough's body flew back, and Sarah's shoulders and head smacked the door with the gun's recoil. But she didn't waste a moment noting the instant headache or certain bruising she'd have. She'd hit him square in the chest and he was down.

Whirling around, she tried to open the front door. But the knob wouldn't turn and the dead bolt wouldn't budge. Codes. Codes! Atticus had mentioned codes. She ran her fingers across the keypad on the door. She had no clue what the unlock codes might be.

The back door! McDonough had come in that way. Either Sandoval had left it unlocked or he'd gotten that information from Officer Burkhardt, too.

Sarah ran, sidling against the wall as she scooted past the sham officer in the middle of the floor. He was stirring now, twisting onto his side, moaning in agony, ripping at his shirtfront. She'd only wounded him. Well, he could bleed to death for all she cared!

She reached the kitchen, spared Mickey a glance, to make sure he was breathing, and a pitying curse before stepping over him and heading for the back door.

"Miss Cartwright!"

What? McDonough sounded angry, not injured.

"Miss Cartwright!"

He was up. Moving. His heavy steps gained speed and purpose as he burst into the kitchen.

Where was the blood?

She reached the back door. Jimmied the knob. It wouldn't open. "Dammit!" She tried the dead bolt. Twisted the lock. "Open, dammit!"

A zillion pinpricks of pain radiated across her scalp as McDonough grabbed a fistful of hair and jerked her away from the door.

Her eyes watered. Her throat clenched with a scream. She swung the gun around but he kicked it from her hand.

"A-a-ah!"

Her wrist throbbing, Sarah clawed at his hand, desperate to free herself. He tossed her toward the center of the room, and she slid helplessly across the smooth linoleum. She crashed into the legs of a chair and knocked it over. As her vision cleared, the bruises registered. But he was coming. Always coming!

"You're a rather good shot, Miss Cartwright. Two bullets, center mass." He'd pulled back enough of his shirt to reveal the flak vest he wore underneath. She'd stunned him, bruised him. She hadn't wounded him at all. "Officer Burkhardt let me borrow this as well as his spare uniform. The police here in Kansas City are so accommodating."

Sarah didn't waste her breath on pleas or protests. She scrambled backward like a crab until she cleared the chair. Then she rolled to her knees, pushed to her feet.

"I'm not happy when things don't go according to plan. But I will get the job done. I will not disappoint Mr. Wolfe." She kicked the chair at him. He dodged it and kept coming toward her. No matter what color his eyes, no matter what face he wore, she'd always know what terror looked like. "If I have to knock you out with my fist, you will come with me."

She grabbed the edge of the table and shoved with all her strength.

He caught it, staggered back a step and shoved it right back.

"No!" Sarah clutched her stomach, curled into a ball

and spun away to absorb the brunt of the blow on her hip. "Don't hurt my baby!"

"What?"

"Please don't hurt my—"

He was stunned. "Whose baby?"

"Mine."

He threw aside the table and grabbed her arm, nearly jerking it from its socket. "Who's the damn father? You were with Teddy that night. Is it his?" The newly healed surgery scars on either side of his nose reddened with his rage. "You bitches! There will be—No. Wolfe. Baby!"

Sarah clawed at the tender skin. When his grip on her loosened, she jabbed her fingers straight into his eyes. He cursed and let go.

An unexpectedly fierce need to protect the innocent life she carried in her womb gave Sarah the reckless strength to shoulder him aside and run toward the living room. If she couldn't open the door, she'd break a window. If she couldn't break a window she'd—

She heard a tornadic rush of wind, the blare of a horn, a clap of thunder a split second before the front wall of the house bowed, cracked and flew into the foyer and hall.

Another explosion? She jumped back. "What the—?"

And then she glimpsed the black fender, the big tires spinning in Reverse.

Coop.

The front of the truck disappeared, and bricks and glass and plaster and wood crashed to the floor, throwing up dust and debris.

Coop!

Sarah covered her mouth and nose, and shielded her eyes as the plaster dust snowed down around her.

And then she saw him, breaking through the hole he'd made with his truck. "Sarah!"

"Coop!"

"You bitch!"

"Get down!"

The bullets started flying and Sarah dropped to the floor and crawled toward the opening. "It's McDonough!"

"C'mon, babe! Move it!" Coop was on his stomach, returning fire. McDonough's path must have been blocked by rubble. Or she'd done some real damage to his eyes. His shots went wide. She scraped her fingers over splintered wood, pinched her foot in a tumbling pile of bricks. "Come on!"

McDonough's cursing abruptly stopped, and she heard footsteps scrabbling through the debris, then running to the back of the house. "He has the lock codes," Sarah warned, pushing herself up onto her hands and knees. "He'll escape out the back."

"Let him run." Coop grabbed a fistful of her shirt and helped pull her through the last few inches. She tumbled into him and clung to his solid, real warmth. But just as quickly, he was pushing her away, pulling her to her feet. "Are you all right?"

She was breathless. Achy. Scared. "Didn't you hear me? McDonough's here."

"So I gather." He scooped her up against his side and climbed out of the pile of debris. When he hit flat ground, he dropped her feet into the cool, wet grass, took her by the hand and ran to his truck. "Let's go."

The hood was smashed, the windshield cracked, the black paint gray with scratches and dust. "Oh, Coop, your poor—"

"Get in!" With little ceremony, he lifted her inside behind the wheel, forcing her to scramble across the seat as he crawled in right behind her. "Move it!"

He laid his gun on the seat between them and forced the wounded truck into gear. He looked over his shoulder and stomped on the gas, backing over the lawn and driveway and curb, following the deep, rutted tracks he'd left in the muddy earth when he'd rammed into the house.

When he hit pavement, he cut the wheel sharply and wrenched it into Drive. Sarah hit the door and bounced, bracing her hands on the dashboard before she landed on the floor. "Cooper Bellamy!"

"Hold on!" He floored it.

Resigned to wild driving and no explanations, Sarah crawled across the seat. She reached over Coop's lap and found the seatbelt to fasten him in. Then she scooted back to the passenger seat and strapped in herself. "How did you know I needed you?"

"I got your call. But I couldn't get into the house. Had to make my own door."

"Sorry about your truck."

"It can be replaced." He pulled his phone off his belt and pushed it across the seat, picking up his gun and keeping it in his hand as he steered onto a blacktop road. "Are you hurt?"

"Banged up. Some cuts and scrapes, but nothing serious. Atticus and Sandoval are inside. Unconscious, but alive. I think Sandoval may have taken a bribe or been duped by McDonough." She couldn't shake the image of cold-eyed rage that had possessed McDonough's face when she'd pleaded to save her baby. She cradled her stomach and cooed a soothing prayer. "I'm sorry, little one. I didn't understand how important you were. Not until now. I'm so sorry."

The truck protested but picked up speed. Coop frowned in her direction as he skidded onto a gravel road. "Is the baby okay?"

"She's fine." *She?* Where had that come from? "At least I think she's a girl. I feel like—" Glancing in the sideview mirror, she caught sight of a police cruiser pulling onto the road a half mile behind them. "Is that McDonough?"

"That'd be my guess. No siren."

"He killed a man. An Officer Burkhardt. That's probably his car."

"Call 9-1-1. Tell them. Give them my name and ask them to patch you through to Captain John Kincaid. Tell him everything you heard or saw in that house." She picked up the phone. "Tell them there are two officers down at the safe house and that they need assistance."

Just as the police cruiser seemed to be gaining, Coop spun completely off the road into a stand of trees.

"Coop!" She grabbed the dash and held on for dear life.

They were going to crash!

He shifted into four-wheel drive as they careened over rocks and splashed through a creek. The truck climbed up the opposite bank before he turned again.

"Where are we going?"

"Away."

She risked a look over her shoulder. There was no sign of the police cruiser behind them. "Did we lose him?"

"That's the idea."

They bounced through a ditch and came up onto an asphalt road. Soon they were driving through a busy residential development. Sarah had no idea where they were, how far they had gone or where they were headed. But she trusted that Coop knew what he was doing. Trusted that he'd keep her and her baby safe.

He nodded toward the phone on the seat between them. "Make the call." He tucked his gun into the back of his belt before reaching across to squeeze her hand.

Sarah looked up into eyes of turbulent—real—blue. "Thank you."

He nodded and turned his eyes back to the street. "That bastard isn't catching us today."

Chapter Nine

"Wake up, sleepyhead. Your turn for the shower."

The weight on the deep, warm bed shifted and Sarah started to roll toward the side. But a pair of big hands caught her and pushed her back to the center.

She snuggled into the smooth cotton pillowcase and murmured, "Just a few more minutes. I'm so tired."

There was a gentle swat on her rump, and a voice she clearly recognized as Coop's leaned in close to her ear. "Up and at 'em, soldier. What do you think this is—a bed-and-breakfast?"

She giggled as she opened her eyes and pushed him away. When he stood up, the mattress righted itself and she regained the leverage to plump the pillows behind her and prop herself up on her elbows. "It happens to be a very nice bed-and-breakfast south of St. Louis, as I recall." Brushing aside the fall of hair that hung over one cheek, Sarah took in the turn-of-the-century decor with its four-poster bed, dark walnut woods, and drapes, rugs and quilts in various shades of lavender and cream. She touched the porcelain wash basin and pitcher on the table beside her, admiring the quality of the well-preserved antique. "This is a converted home once owned by an entrepreneur who helped develop the state's mining industry. It has been restored with historical accuracy and modern conveniences, to attract both tourists and couples whose trucks have crashed through brick walls and can't go any farther. So, yes, sir—" she saluted her wiseacre alarm clock "—I think I'm in a bed-and-breakfast, and I'm taking advantage of the bed part."

"You cheated," he winked, hitching his jeans up over his shorts and zipping them. "You read the brochure."

Sarah looked away as an instant awareness heated her cheeks. If she'd known Coop was parading around in nothing more than those long, muscular legs and underwear, she'd have been wide awake a whole lot sooner.

She feigned an intense interest in the child's portrait etched in ink beneath the pitcher's glaze. "I can't believe I'm asleep in the middle of the afternoon."

"Try 7:00 p.m. You were dozing in the truck before we got here. It was all I could do to get us checked in and up the stairs before you fell into that bed and went off to dream land again."

"No wonder I'm so hungry." She pulled the quilts up to her chin to mask the growling protests in her stomach. "Is there someplace we can go out and get dinner in this town?"

The foolishness of her words registered the instant she uttered them.

"We can't go out, Sarah."

"Of course. I wasn't thinking." Here she was worrying about naps and food. She wrinkled the quilt in her fists, and sought out Coop at the dresser across the room. Now she could see that he'd tucked his gun into the back waist-band of his jeans. The fear that she'd worn like a cloak from the moment Atticus Kincaid had stumbled into the john that morning settled around her again. "Are we safe? McDonough didn't follow us here, did he?"

Coop pulled a T-shirt from the top drawer and hooked it over one of the bedposts before sitting on the edge of the bed again. He unwound her fingers from the quilt and gently rubbed them between his hands. "Relax. I lost McDonough before we even hit the city limit sign. It helps to be a native and know where all the back roads are."

"Is there any way to trace us here? Could someone spot your truck and report it? Even if it's a call to the local sheriff, someone could pick up the report in Kansas City, couldn't they?"

"If they broadcast it statewide and they know what they're looking for, sure." He reached out to brush that pesky crimp of slept-on hair off her face again. "But nobody's going to recognize that pretty face here. This is a small town, packed with plenty of tourists during the fall for wine-tastings and holiday shopping at the craft places—or just to get away from the city for the weekend. A couple of extra strangers will get lost in the crowd, just like everybody else. We'll be fine here for a little while—long enough to get our bearings and rest up so we're sharp. I've been awake for the better part of two days, and I know it's been rough for you."

"Rough for me? What about that poor officer that McDonough killed? And his family?" Sarah shook her head, clutching Coop's fingers to halt the massage she didn't deserve." "Who knows who he'll hurt next, trying to get to me? I shouldn't be complaining."

"Hey." Coop nudged her under the chin and demanded that she look at him. "You are not responsible for the crimes he commits. You're the woman who's going to put him away forever, remember? Kansas City will be a safer place because you've got the guts to stand up in court and tell the truth."

Those deep blue eyes had a lot of faith in her. Maybe more than she had in herself. "I'll tell the truth—if we ever catch him."

"McDonough will eventually make a mistake and we'll catch him." But his pep talk was an honest one, not full of false hope. "I've already been on the phone with Captain Kincaid. They found Roger Burkhardt's body. Unfortunately, they also found the squad car and spare uniform that McDonough took. So he's changed himself again. There's an APB out for him, but who knows what disguise we should be looking for next?"

"I'll know him when I see him." The certainty of that went as deep as the chill in her bones.

Coop nodded, accepting the grim pronouncement. "By the way, they found two bullet holes in the discarded uniform. Burkhardt had his throat slashed, never even got his gun out of his holster. If Kincaid and Sandoval were unconscious, then who…?"

"I shot McDonough. I didn't know he was wearing a vest."

"*You* shot Shaw McDonough?"

"Yes." She shrugged, a little perturbed by his incredulity. "Yes, already. I keep trying to tell people I'm not some helpless, naive little girl. I'm twenty-seven years old. I grew up in a house with two cops and have a dad who doesn't always associate with the nicest of people. I've been around guns most of my life. For my own safety, and everyone else's, doesn't it make sense that I would know how to use one? And Mom and Seth both said that if you're in danger, a good cop doesn't aim to wound a man, they aim to stop him. I aimed for his heart and I tried to stop him."

"Down, girl." Coop was grinning by the time she'd finished venting. "You know, the only way you could be any sexier to me at this moment is if you drop that quilt and give me a glimpse of those sexy pjs I know you're wearing."

How could a woman *not* laugh when Cooper Bellamy turned on the charm?

"You're shameless!" She batted at his bare shoulder. "It's not my fault I look like I should be hanging in a hunting lodge. Apparently, that safehouse was set up for male witnesses. This was the only pair of pajamas they had."

"I'm not complaining." He kissed her once, then arched a wicked eyebrow. "I like the view."

He looked down through the shirt's gaping cleavage. All the way down to her belly button.

"Oh! You!" Sarah clutched the collar together at her neck, blocking Coop's hungry gaze.

But then he kissed her again. One of *those* kisses that made her forget secrets and shames, and dimmed the nightmares of killers and death. And suddenly, she was holding on to Coop's shoulders, not the pjs. Instead of stiff flannel, her palms slid over supple skin. Instead of clinging to the flimsy quilt, her fingers clung to corded muscle and sinew. Instead of lying on the bed, she was lying on top of Coop.

Her toes curled into the soft denim at his knees. Her nose inhaled the steamy heat of the shower that lingered in the hills and hollows of his naked chest. Her lips molded to the persuasive seduction of his.

She was with Coop, and all was right with the world.

Until a knock at the door made every liquid muscle inside her tense again.

She gasped and lifted her head, her gaze going straight to the lock on the suite door.

"Shh. Easy, babe." The hands that had roamed at will beneath her shirt now came up to gently frame her face. "It's okay."

"How do you know?"

"Because the bad guys don't knock."

She thought back to that morning, standing over an unconscious man, pointing a gun at the bathroom door, waiting for the terror on the other side. "Shaw McDonough did."

"Hey." Coop sat up, spilling her into his lap. The intimacy of the embrace had passed and Sarah shivered with a chill that attacked her from the inside out. "Hey."

His eyes and touch and patience waited for her to read the sincerity in his expression.

"Where's that tough girl who shoots to kill? Trust me a little, okay? I'm expecting a friend. No one will hurt you. Not while I'm around. I promise."

She pressed her hand over the strong, steady beat of his heart. If he wasn't alarmed, then she shouldn't be.

Still, she flinched when the knock sounded again. This time, a man's voice followed the knock. "Coop? You decent?"

"Coming." Sarah crawled off his lap and he rolled his legs over the side of the bed.

"Who's that? One of those tourists who's helping us blend in with the crowd?"

"This, milady—" he hopped up with a grin that made her fears recede even further "—is how I can afford this fancy place." He opened the door and greeted a tall man with silver hair that needed to see a comb. Then he turned and winked at Sarah. "I get the favorite nephew discount."

"Don't tell your brothers that. They both think they're my favorite." The man wrinkled his nose in a hands-free effort to push his thick, black-framed glasses higher on his face. He carried a tray of food on one arm and a stack of clothing and supplies in the other. She saw a remarkably familiar expression on his kind face as he politely looked past the rumpled bed and grinned at Sarah. "Hi. I'm Walt."

"Hi." Sarah made sure her pajama top covered everything but the blush on her cheeks, and slid off the bed. "Sorry we didn't get the door right away."

"No problem. I know how this guy operates." He turned and shoved his parcels toward Coop. "Here. You have to earn that favorite nephew discount. Make yourself useful."

"But I'm a guest."

"You're family. Now introduce me to this pretty

lady." Coop willingly took the load from his uncle's arms and nudged the door shut behind them. Sarah noted that, despite the friendly banter, he took the time to lock it, as well. "Walter Bellamy, meet Sarah Cartwright. He's my favorite uncle."

"I'm your only uncle, but I appreciate the thought."

"Walt runs this fine establishment."

"This fine money pit, you mean. Depending on what breaks down on any given day." Like that devilish grin. A sense of humor was clearly a family trait.

Sarah wondered if Coop would have shared that same thick head of hair, too—before his battle with cancer.

"I think it's beautiful," Sarah said, including in her compliment both that handsome bald pate and the colors of the room. "From what I've seen so far, at any rate. Very cozy and comfortable."

"See?" Walt pointed a finger at his nephew. "I told you she'd like this room. I know women."

"She was half-asleep when we came in. She would have liked an army cot."

"Well, if given a choice…" Sarah grinned and the men laughed, reminding her of *fun* and *normal* and the life she'd nearly lost today.

But she hadn't, thanks to the *favorite nephew* who dumped the clothes, some toiletries and a first-aid kit onto the bed. He pulled a carrot stick off the tray and popped it into his mouth while Sarah apologized for her appearance. "Normally, I don't run around the countryside looking like this."

"Coop said you might need to borrow some clothes. I've got some things a lady friend of mine left here. They may not be the latest fashion, but at least they'll curve in all the right places. I brought a few different pieces to try. Hope you can find something that fits."

"Thank you."

Walt stole the tray from Coop when he picked up half of one sandwich and started to eat it, too. "Didn't I teach you any better than that? Ladies first."

"Well, you two were talking," he said around a cheekful of food.

Sarah couldn't help but feel the love and energy in the room. Being around the Bellamys was an awful lot like being around her fourth-graders at recess. She'd certainly have to be on her toes to keep up with this team. "Thanks for putting us up. Or should I say putting up with us?"

"I see you know Cooper well. Trust me, it's no problem." Walt grinned. "Well, I'll leave you two alone. If you need anything else, just holler."

"Hey, Walt," Coop called out, while Sarah perched on the edge of the bed and picked up one of the sandwiches and a can of lemon-lime soda. Coop excused himself and walked his uncle out the door. "I need to talk to you about getting some wheels."

After a reassuring click of the lock, Sarah polished off the sandwich and a handful of crudités. If she had ever longed for excitement in her life, she needn't look any farther than a herd of Bellamys together in the same room.

A few minutes later, with her stomach full and her body relatively rested, she decided to tackle the last step toward feeling as normal as possible under the circumstances. She stripped off the hideous pajamas she'd been wearing for nearly twenty-four hours and went into the bathroom to run the hot water for a shower. Taking shampoo, shower gel and a washcloth with her, Sarah stepped into the claw-footed tub, pulled the curtain around the circular bar and pushed the lever to let the steamy spray wash the grit and stress from her hair and skin.

But as she dabbed at the scrapes and cuts on her feet, the bloom of a purplish red bruise on her calf caught her eye and she paused. There was a similar mark—bluer, darker—on her left knee and a matching swelling on her right knee from when she'd hit the floor of the safe house kitchen and skidded. She counted the welts along her thigh that matched the rungs of the chair she'd hit when Shaw McDonough had picked her up by the hair and tossed her across the room—treating her with the same hateful disdain he'd shown Dawn Kingsley when he'd taken her out with the trash.

The water cooled and she turned it off. But there was still hot moisture on Sarah's cheeks when she stepped out of the shower and wiped the fog off the mirror. She combed her hair out, straight and slick against her scalp, wincing at every tug. But it was the memory of the violence, the cold-eyed hate in Shaw McDonough's eyes—as much as the pain itself that let hot tears overflow and drip onto her naked breasts.

"Oh, my God."

There were bruises there, too, but none as large and dark and sinister as the fist-sized bruise that covered her right hipbone.

Sarah splayed her fingers over the fullness of her belly where her little one was growing. So small, so innocent.

That injury from the table—rammed straight at her womb. If she hadn't turned at that last second…if she hadn't shielded herself from McDonough's attack…

Coop found her like that, staring in the mirror, unaware of her nakedness. Her eyes red and glistening with tears. Cradling her belly. Quiet.

"Sarah?"

She looked too fragile to touch, too frightened to reach.

He'd seen her bravely tell him a hurtful truth, be sick to her stomach and exhausted without complaining. She'd stood up to her father and been kind when he didn't deserve it. He'd watched her chase after a madman and dive to the floor with bullets flying—but none of that scared him as much as the eerie, lost pain reflected in her pale, battered body.

"Talk to me, sweetheart."

She couldn't look away from her reflection. "He wanted to kill my baby. He said he wanted her dead."

Coop's hands fisted at his side as one tear spilled over. And then another.

He forced open his hands as an even tighter fist squeezed around his heart.

"I love her, Coop. More than I ever knew. And he wants to kill her."

Smooth-talking Cooper Bellamy didn't have the words to say what he felt. All he had was his faith in her strength and the love in his heart.

Before the next tear fell, he scooped her up in his arms and carried her to the bed. There, he set her on the edge and knelt in front of her, quickly tending to the wounds that needed salve and a bandage. He dabbed cooling alcohol on the angriest of her bruises and then retrieved his clean T-shirt from the bedpost. He slipped it over her head, then pulled her arms through the sleeves. He covered her breasts and then stopped, feeling a need inside him so powerful that it made no logical sense.

He leaned forward and tenderly kissed her belly, claiming Sarah and her baby as his own. "Nobody's hurting either one of you. Not while there's breath in my body."

"Oh, Coop." Her fingers were strong and welcoming against his scalp as she held him there. Against her. Against her baby. Her lips brushed the top of his head. "This should be your child. I wish…I wish…"

He lifted his mouth and silenced her despair with a kiss.

He might never understand what had driven her to sleep with a man like Teddy Wolfe. But it didn't matter anymore. His pride was the only thing that had taken a real hit, and he'd learned a long time ago that when he was fighting for his life—fighting for the things that really mattered—pride wasn't nearly as important as faith and hope…and love. He loved Sarah Cartwright. And he'd fallen in love with her baby, too.

"I know, sweetheart," he finally said. "I wish it, too."

Despite her long nap, Sarah's emotions had finally exhausted her. Coop lay her back on the pillows and pulled his shirt down to cover her. He made sure the door was locked, checked his gun and set it on the table beside the bed. Then he unsnapped the top button of his jeans and crawled in beside her.

He gathered Sarah in his arms and she snuggled back

into that place she fit so perfectly—against his chest, tucked beneath his chin, his body cocooned around hers. She laced her fingers through his and drew his hand to her belly.

He'd tried to laugh her out of her fears, tried to kiss them away. But in the end, there was only one thing he could do.

He held her.

He held them.

And together, they slept.

"MR. WOLFE." SHAW MCDONOUGH breathed through the defensive spike in his temper as he closed the hotel door behind him to find Theodore Wolfe and two other men making themselves at home in his suite. "This is a surprise."

He never had liked surprises.

Especially like the one at the safe house yesterday morning. Not only was Sarah Cartwright awake and able to fight back, inconveniencing his carefully orchestrated murder and disposal setup, but she claimed she was pregnant.

That moved her elimination to the top of his organizational planning list. Even ahead of whatever bit of business his British boss wanted him to take care of now.

"Shaw. Congratulations on maintaining your standard of living—right under the noses of the local constabulary." He nodded toward Shaw's red-and-white running suit. "Though I can't say much for the tailoring here in the States."

The track suit provided the perfect cover to smuggle

the supplies he was carrying into the hotel. Plus, the loose fit hid the bruises and swelling from the bullets the Cartwright bitch had fired at him this morning.

"I've always been good about putting away money. And staying in fighting shape." He lowered his chin in a bow. "I learned from the best."

Theodore Wolfe laughed from his seat at the very desk where Shaw had outlined his plans, tracked the Cartwrights' schedules and built the remote-trigger bomb he'd placed in Seth Cartwright's car. The sixty-something Wolfe puffed on an imported cigar, his thumb tucked inside the vest of his three-piece suit, looking every bit the aristocratic businessman he claimed to be.

But Shaw knew him better than that. He and Wolfe were too much alike for him not to recognize a predator when he saw one. Teddy had never had that perception about people. Whatever they could do for him, he took—without ever really knowing what it might cost him in return.

Teddy had never pegged Seth Cartwright as an undercover cop running security for his casino. He'd never taken Rebecca Page's curious questions seriously, not even when she'd found the evidence needed to prove that Wolfe International—that Shaw himself with Teddy *supervising*—had killed her father. Teddy had seen Dawn Kingsley—the gold-digging tramp—as wife and mother material.

Shaw had seen the truths Teddy never could. That's why *he* deserved to be Theodore Wolfe's heir. He was more like his boss than his own son ever had been. It was also the reason he had to be particularly careful about his words and actions—even nuances of expression—around Theodore, Sr.

"I'd say make yourself at home, but I see you've already helped yourself to the brandy and cigars." Shaw crossed to the closet and slid open the door, setting the football bag he carried over his arm inside and shutting the door. True, he kept himself in shape, but he hadn't been anywhere near a soccer pitch that evening. Still, it was a reasonable enough cover that no one suspected he carried explosives and firearms instead of sports equipment inside. Shaw gestured to the decanter sitting on the corner of the desk. "Do you mind?"

"Help yourself."

Shaw poured himself a brandy, bringing him close enough to assess what arms, if any, the other two men carried on them. He immediately identified the sidearm bulging beneath the jacket of the thick-necked thug standing behind Wolfe. He wore a piece at the ankle, too. He was the bodyguard. The other man, with darker skin, was familiar enough. He recognized him as a doctor from the clinic where Wolfe had sent him to change his face. The doctor wouldn't be armed with anything more dangerous than a scalpel. Neither man was a threat to Shaw with the weapons he carried and his expertise at using them.

Knowing that Wolfe always wore a Beretta at his back as well, Shaw relaxed enough to pull up a chair and sit.

"Aren't you taking a risk by showing up in Kansas City so soon after Teddy's unfortunate death?" He took a sip to smooth over the way *unfortunate* stuck in his throat.

Theodore leaned forward and tapped the ash from his

cigar into the ashtray. "My informant at KCPD tells me that you've moved up on their Most Wanted list ahead of me. Besides, what can they pin on me? Grieving for my son's death? That's no crime. I understand they're going to release some of Teddy's things from evidence soon, as well. As far as the Americans are concerned, I'm simply here to retrieve some family heirlooms."

"Well, I'm not so naive to assume you've come across the Atlantic Ocean and half the U.S. to pay me a social call." He swirled the brandy at the bottom of the snifter, inhaled its rich, spicy scent and drank half of it. The liquid heat burned down his throat and sharpened his senses before he asked, "What business do we need to discuss?"

"I understand your need for closure and that your very survival may depend upon eliminating the eyewitness to Dawn Kingsley's murder."

"Yes…?" No way in hell would he let the bitch and her bastard child live one moment longer than was necessary. It was just a matter of finding her, now that she'd gone into hiding with that bald American cowboy friend of hers. But he *would* find her.

"I want you to delay her execution."

Shaw got up and paced off the length of the suite's main room. He downed the last of the alcohol in one swallow. "I told you Seth Cartwright would be dead soon enough. I've already established an identity and work permit at the hospital where he's recuperating. I'll finish him off one evening—even while the guard stands outside his door. You instructed me to make his family suffer, and I haven't failed you. You should see the grieving mother and his despairing fiancée."

"I'm glad to hear that. But this visit isn't about avenging Teddy's death." Wolfe looked to the man of ethnic descent who'd been sitting quietly near the window. "You remember Dr. Rajiv from your surgery down in the islands?"

"He was on the staff at the clinic there. You're not going to change my appearance again, are you? The new skin still itches from those grafts."

Rajiv pushed to his feet. "There is an ointment…"

Mr. Wolfe held up his hand and the doctor fell dutifully silent. "Dr. Rajiv is more than a general surgeon. Like the other staff at my private clinic, I require multiple specialties. He has also studied obstetrics and gynecology."

"Well, I'm certainly not having a baby, am I." Shaw faked a laugh he didn't feel, and the others in the room joined in.

Until Theodore Wolfe ground out his cigar and stopped laughing. "I believe Sarah Cartwright is."

The brandy soured in Shaw's stomach. It took all his considerable will to maintain a quizzical expression. "I killed the woman I loved for you. I have no qualms about killing an unborn baby."

"I have no qualms about you carrying out any task I assign you," Wolfe assured him. But Shaw wasn't really feeling it. "Dr. Rajiv can administer an amnio test to determine the baby's father before it's born. It can be a risky procedure, but I want her to have the test to see if Teddy is the father."

Everything inside Shaw braced. He set the brandy snifter down and walked away before he crushed the crystal glass in his fist. "If Miss Cartwright *is* pregnant, what makes you think the baby is Teddy's?"

"A rather indebted little bird told me."

"What does that mean?"

Mr. Wolfe nodded toward the thick-necked thug who crossed to the door and went into the hall. A moment later he came back with a familiar face. Shaw ran his tongue along the inside of his teeth, hoping Mr. Wolfe would give him the order to off this idiot, as well. He'd been a detriment to their American partnership from the moment the Riverboat Casino had opened. But Teddy had been so sure they could manipulate his weakness to control him and use him as a scapegoat for their illegal activities if they were caught.

"Shaw?" the man said, squinting at the new contours of his face. "Is that you? I wouldn't have recognized you if—"

"Austin Cartwright." Shaw hated friendly chitchat as much as he loathed surprises.

Theodore stood, resting a hand on Shaw's shoulder. "I had a very interesting phone call from Mr. Cartwright a few days ago. I paid him a large sum of money for the information he shared with me." He turned to Austin. "Tell Shaw what you told me."

"My daughter's pregnant. She's a good girl—not a slut, by any means. I know of only one man she's slept with in the past few years."

"And who was that man?"

"Your son. Teddy."

Shaw hadn't needed this kind of confirmation. He'd already seen the truth in the woman's eyes when she'd thought her child was in danger. She'd been more afraid for the baby than herself. And he'd wanted her dead all the more because of it.

But the worst news for Shaw was good news for Theodore Wolfe. "I'm changing my orders. This is no longer a kill assignment. I want Austin's daughter brought to me alive. And I want Dr. Rajiv to perform his test on her."

Shaw couldn't look at the old man. He couldn't risk betraying his real intent. "Kidnapping is more difficult than murder. It's not as clean. What if someone tries to play hero? What if she fights back? She might be killed, anyway."

Wolfe's hand was on his shoulder again, demanding that he face him. "Don't let that happen. If I have a grandchild, I want him. You can do whatever you want to Miss Cartwright *after* the baby is in my hands."

"What? Hold on there. You said my daughter would be safe!" Was Austin Cartwright finally growing a backbone? Now that was worth a real laugh. But the thick-necked bruiser restrained him the instant he moved toward Wolfe.

"She'll be safe enough," Wolfe assured him, never once flinching at the verbal or physical threats. "Until the baby is born."

"But I thought—"

Shaw took the privilege of silencing Austin's whine with a punch to the gut. He crumpled to the floor, moaning.

He brushed off his hands before turning to his boss. "What if it's impossible to extricate her from protective custody without harming her or the baby?"

"That's why I'm here to offer my assistance, Shaw." By assistance, he meant supervision. That meant unwelcome interference with his plans. "And just so you don't decide to put your interests before mine, you and I are going to work as a team."

Chapter Ten

Though her dreams had been troubling—with images of running and running, of her stomach being cut open, of a baby lying still and silent in her arms—Sarah awoke feeling more rested and less queasy than she had in weeks. If she didn't have a hitman after her with a loathing for women and an inexplicable hatred for her baby, she might actually think she felt good this morning.

A big breakfast, courtesy of Walt Bellamy's gourmet talents, helped. As did the clean set of clothes. True, she had to roll the loose-fitting khakis up at the ankle, and the untucked blouse and sweater hung down to her thighs. But the tennis shoes and underwear fit and made her feel a little more shielded from eyes and the elements than she had running around barefoot in those atrocious jammies.

The only thing missing from this cozy morning in the kitchen was Coop. And he'd disappeared before she'd dressed and come down to join Walt for waffles and bacon.

Not that Coop's uncle wasn't good company. She butted him aside from the sink with her hip when he tried to push his way in. "You cooked. I don't mind doing the dishes."

"Yes, but you're my guest."

"I thought we were family."

"Cooper is family—he can do the grunt work. You, little one, are my guest. Now sit and let an old man spoil you a bit." He gave Sarah a towel to dry her hands and took her by the elbow to guide her back to the kitchen table and the herbal tea he'd prepared for her.

"Well, do you mind if I at least sit here and keep you company?"

Walt dipped his arms elbow-deep into the sudsy water. "I'd love it. You have a kind heart to indulge an old man like me. I see what my nephew likes about you—beyond the obvious, of course."

The obvious? Like shadows under her eyes? Mood swings? Sudden nap attacks and the need for food right on the dot six times a day?

"Where is Coop, by the way?" She'd already scoured their suite and as much of the house as Walt would let her see, looking for him. Coop had wakened her with a kiss and told her he had some things to do. *"Get dressed and go down to the kitchen to meet Uncle Walt for breakfast. I'll be back soon."*

But *soon* had been a couple of hours ago, and while she certainly felt no threat from Walt Bellamy and his hospitality, she worried about what Coop might be doing. She worried about Coop, period.

"He said he had to make a couple of phone calls and run some errands. Since his truck is on its last hubcap, I arranged for a friend to rent him a new one."

"But they'll trace his credit card."

Walt winked away her flare of concern. "Like I said—it's a friend of mine. He'll take cash."

Sarah breathed a little easier. "I thought Coop was a military brat and moved around a lot, until he lost his dad and the rest of the family settled in Kansas City. Does he know his way around here?"

"Oh, yeah." Walt pulled the last pan from the water and squeezed out the dishcloth to wipe down the countertops. "No matter where they lived, Coop and his brothers and sisters spent their summers with me whenever their father was deployed. It gave their mom a break from single-parenting, and I suppose I provided some kind of adult male role model. Though I must have seemed like a cantankerous old coot compared to the fine man my brother—their father—was."

"I haven't met the others, but I can tell that Coop loves you very much."

"Yeah. It's mutual. But don't you go tellin' him that, though." He pointed a bony finger at Sarah, and she smiled at its harmless intent. "He might very well be my favorite nephew, but I don't want it to go to his shiny head."

He kept talking as he finished cleaning up. "But I am proud of him, with the way he stepped up to help raise his brothers and sisters and the way he took on cancer. Just like his dad was—storm the beach. Attack the enemy. Hide what you're really feeling so the fear doesn't become another enemy." Walt poured himself a cup of coffee and joined her at the table. "Sure, that charm and sense of humor is a natural Bellamy trait. It's easier—more supportive, maybe—to be around people who laugh and smile, instead of worrying themselves to death about a daddy in a war zone or a son diagnosed with cancer."

Walt reached across the table and rested his hand on top of Sarah's. "But when that boy gets serious, that's when you know he's really feeling something deep. And though I can tell he likes to make you laugh, I've never seen him be as serious around anybody as I've seen him with you."

Serious, as in kissing her belly and holding her through the night? Being there to quietly soothe her through her nightmares? Serious as in putting his life on the line to keep her safe?

Sarah turned her hand to latch on to Walt's. "Coop is very special to me, too. He's been there for me in a lot of ways—when no one else could, or wanted to be."

Walt pushed his glasses up onto the bridge of his nose and studied her as intently as though she were a specimen beneath a microscope. Finally, she could feel the heat warming her cheeks and she dropped her gaze to the table. "What?"

"When you say 'special,' do you mean Coop's just a special friend—or that he means something…special… to you?"

Sarah pulled away at the probing intensity of his question. She wrapped her hands around her mug of tea and hid the turbulent response of her thoughts behind a long, warm swallow of the fragrant brew.

Walt sat back in his chair, his genial expression momentarily transformed into a protective fatherly scowl that she wished her own father had shown on her behalf.

"Cooper might have a knack for rollin' with the punches life throws at him better than any man I know. But just because he's grinning on the outside doesn't mean he isn't hurting on the inside. That doesn't mean he can't feel things deeply. I don't want to see that boy get hurt."

Sarah lifted her gaze and met Walt's straight on. Of that much she was certain. "I don't want Coop to be hurt, either. He's definitely a friend and I care about him a lot. I don't know how I could have gotten through these past few days without him. But I'm not sure I deserve him. I did something once that did…hurt him. And I will regret that for the rest of my life. I don't know if he can ever truly forgive me—deep inside, like you said. Even if I did say…I loved him…he might not believe me."

Walt nodded, accepting that she understood the precarious balance between needing Coop—even wanting Coop—and accepting the responsibility of loving the man. "I think you have a good heart in you, Sarah Cartwright. Just be sure about how you feel before you make any promises. And darlin'?" He leaned forward, pried her fingers from her mug and held on tightly. "It's your actions that will convince that boy you love him. More than words. It's what people *do* that will make you believe he forgives you, and make him believe in your love."

"I do love him, Walt."

It was a realization she hadn't been entirely sure of until she'd said the words out loud. Once upon a time she'd thought she wanted a man who was cultured and worldly and debonair—a man with the means and power to sweep her away from her mundane existence and the heavy responsibility of taking care of a father who was really no father at all. But now she knew it wasn't the wealth or travel or lifestyle that could take her to a safer, saner place.

It was a man.

It was Cooper Bellamy.

But the realization was too new to quite know what to do with it right now. Carrying another man's—a criminal's—baby hurt Coop deeply. It was a blow to his manhood. His pride. To the trust he had in her. How did she make that up to him? How could she prove that *she* had no desire to ever make that kind of mistake about a man again?

It would probably require some of those actions Walt had mentioned.

On impulse, Sarah got up and circled the table. She reached around Walt's shoulders and hugged him tight. "I wish my dad had been more like you. That he knew how to listen…how to care…that he knew how to butt his nose into the business of the people he loved. The Bellamys are lucky to have you." She pulled back, smiling at the blush that stained his cheeks. "I'll think about what you said."

Walt reached up and patted her hand on his shoulder. "Have faith, little one. Take care of my boy. Just like I know he's taking good care of you. It'll work out. If it's meant to be, it'll work out."

The back door squeaked open and shut before Walt could stand. Suddenly, Coop was there, standing in the archway to the kitchen, his gaze darting back and forth between Sarah and his uncle.

"Oh, nice." He walked straight to the coffeepot and poured himself a cup. "I leave this place for an hour, and when I come back you're hittin' on my girl."

Walt pushed back his chair and stood, giving him the same guff right back. "I have to keep in practice, son."

"Well, find your own girl to practice on." Coop took off his ball cap—this one was red for the St. Louis Cardinals instead of his familiar black KCPD cap—and stuffed it into his jacket pocket. His assessing gaze paused on Sarah before he looked to his uncle. "Is everything all right?"

"Everything's fine. Did you have any problem getting the truck?"

"No. It was a good lead. I appreciate it. You sure you won't have any problem ditching my truck?"

Walt shook his head. "I'll take care of that." He crossed to the walk-in pantry and pulled out a large cooler and set it on the table. "I packed the things you asked for. Food, supplies, a charged phone, a backup clip for your Glock. And here are the keys to the cabin." He fished a ring of keys from his pocket and held them up before dropping them into Coop's outstretched hand. "I've already called Kenny Sterling. He'll go out this morning to fire up the generator and make sure the water's running. You might have to air things out, but at least you'll have heat, a flush toilet and privacy."

"Sounds like I'm in the middle of a spy movie. We're not staying here?" Sarah asked, wondering if she'd ever feel a sense of home and permanency again.

Coop's expression was a mix of tough cop and gentle apology. "It's probably a good idea to keep moving for a few days, until someone can get a bead on McDonough. Walt has a cabin not too far south of here, near Mark Twain National Forest. Down there, McDonough won't just be trying to find his way around another country. If he should manage to track us to this side of the state, with the hills and trees and rocks and caves down that way, he's gonna think he's on a whole different planet. That should give us a definite advantage."

Sarah hugged her arms around her waist, understanding the logic of the idea while hating the necessity of it. "That sounds like a good plan. But is there any way we can get word to Mom or Seth about what we're doing? I'm sure they must be crazy with worry right now."

"Too many calls can be risky. They could already be tracing the pings on the cell towers and narrowing down the search."

"The police could—or the FBI. But McDonough? How would he have access to that kind of technology?"

Coop's expression was all cop now. "I think Wolfe International has an inside man on KCPD. Either they've paid someone off to feed them the information they need, or McDonough's disguise is good enough that he's infiltrated the department himself."

Sarah sank into a chair. "Oh, my God. He could be anybody, then. A patrolman. Someone on the technical team. He could even be part of the task force."

Coop set his coffee on the table and came around to kneel beside her. He swallowed her hands up in his. "It doesn't matter who it is, okay? We're going to be smarter and tougher, right?"

She framed his jaw between her hands and smiled,

marveling at his confidence and strength—maybe even absorbing a little of it herself. "Right."

She leaned forward and kissed him, quickly and briefly, considering their audience. But still, the gesture seemed to startle—then please him.

"Thank you for last night," she whispered. Then, raising her voice so Walt could hear and Coop would believe, she stood. "I'm feeling much better this morning. Just tell me what you need me to do."

Coop stood, too, towering beside her. "Well, for one thing, you can quit flirting with my uncle, and for another—" he pulled the cell phone off his belt and pushed it into her hands "—you can call your mother. Keep it short and don't mention our location or destination. But you can tell her you're okay and that I'm on the job."

"Thanks." Her smile included Walt as well. "Thank you, both."

"Get to it, woman," Coop instructed. "By the time I'm done loading up the truck, I expect you to be ready to roll."

"Shh."

Coop watched Sarah's green eyes pop open, full of fear, above the muzzle of his hand. But he couldn't afford to have her cry out if a noise startled her awake, or if she woke up once she realized he wasn't warming the bed beside her and called out to him.

The moment of fear quickly passed. She nodded, understanding the need to remain quiet as he pulled away his hand and let her sit up on the wrought-iron bed. *What is it?* her eyes asked.

"Get in the closet," he whispered against her ear. "I

heard someone walking around outside. I need to check it out."

"How could anyone find us—?"

He shushed her with a finger over her lips. Then he replaced the finger with a quick kiss and pushed the extra Smith & Wesson Walt had packed for him into her hands. She got up and padded along beside him in her stockinged feet, pausing only when she heard the footsteps walking outside, circling behind the back porch, too.

Her fingers dug into the sleeve of his jacket—her only outward sign of fear—before she dutifully walked into the only place without a window in the small lakeside cabin. As she hunkered down out of sight in the shadows of the storage closet, Coop gave her one last set of instructions. "Shoot anybody who comes through this door that isn't me. Got it?"

Sarah nodded. Her skin was pale enough that it glowed in the moonlight, which filtered through the cabin's thick windows. But her grip on the gun was strong, her eyes clear and bright. "Go."

He pulled his own weapon as he closed the door on her. He'd hoped that this place was secluded enough on the lake that they could go two or three days without any contact with the outside world. But maybe that had been wishful thinking. Theodore Wolfe was one of the wealthiest men in the world—and Shaw McDonough one of the smartest. Coop would be a fool to think that he could evade them for very long.

Footsteps in the wet leaves outside a secluded cabin in the middle of the night? Not a good sign. He'd like to think it was just a deer or maybe a bear that hadn't gone into hibernation yet, out scrounging for food.

But he'd heard only one pair of feet walking. Not two. And unless he'd missed learning something about the evolutionary scheme of things, wild animals didn't walk up to shed doors and check padlocks, either.

With the intruder wandering around the back of the cabin, trying to get a glimpse inside the shed to the truck he'd parked there, Coop snuck out the front. He had a gun to the older man's temple before he ever heard Coop coming.

"I'll take that." Coop took the rifle from the intruder and encouraged him to put his hands on top of his fluorescent-orange hunting cap. He ordered the man to slowly turn around while Coop finally turned on the flashlight he carried with him to study his leathery face. "Who are you? You have any ID on you?"

"Kenny Sterling." He turned and spat a stream of tobacco juice into the wet leaves at his feet. "My wallet's in my truck—about a half mile up the road, so you'll just have to take my word for it. I was checkin' to see if you folks got settled in okay. Makin' sure it was you and not trespassers. Now be careful with Gladys there." He inclined his head toward the hunting rifle Coop laid on the ground behind him.

"Gladys will be just fine," Coop answered, neither lowering his gun nor backing away. "Are you in the habit of snooping around in the middle of the night on other people's property?"

"Well, now, don't go gettin' your knickers in a twist. I was out huntin' 'til after dark. Then I went home because the missus expects me to show up for supper or else she gets cranky. This was the soonest I could get out here." Kenny scratched at the stubble on his jaw and then spat again. "'Sides, I got a call from your uncle. Seems he's havin' trouble connectin' to your cell out here. But he said it was important."

That much was true. He'd already tried calling Captain Kincaid to give him an update on his location, but the cell towers were too far away for a signal to cut through the hills and rock in the area.

Coop lowered his gun and picked up Gladys, although he still waited to give the rifle back. "What was Walt's message?"

"Can I put my hands down?"

"What was the message?"

Kenny left his hands on his head, respecting if not appreciating Coop's caution. "Somethin' about a call he got from a man named Austin. Said they knew about his place, and that they were on their way. I'll be damned if I know who *they* are, or what it means. But that's what Walt said."

"He called you?"

"Yeah."

"And you came straight here to warn me?"

"Well, yeah. That's the neighborly thing to—"

"Straight here? Son of a bitch."

Coop holstered his weapon and picked up Gladys. He'd been so worried about protecting Sarah and the baby that he hadn't fully considered the collateral damage to anyone who might try to help him. Though Kenny Sterling seemed to be low-key enough that nothing startled him, his eyes were wide as Coop grabbed his arm and steered him back toward the gravel road, where he claimed to have parked his truck. Coop hurried him along, dumping the cartridges from his rifle as they went.

"What are you doing?"

"Hope you don't mind my taking the precaution." He handed him the empty rifle. "It's not that easy to trust a stranger."

Kenny nodded, needing a push to maintain Coop's brisk pace. "That's good advice—"

"How well do you know my uncle?"

"Well enough, I suppose. I've been watchin' his place in the off season for two years now. Since I retired."

"Good. I need you to get back to your house or the nearest phone and call Walt. Tell him to get out. Now."

"Get out of what?"

"He'll know. Will you make the call?"

"Sure. But—"

"Go! The nearest phone. As fast as you can."

Coop left Kenny at the road, muttering something about crazy city folk. He ran back to the cabin, back to Sarah, praying every step of the way that Kenny Sterling was a man of his word. Praying the old coot would pick up the pace. Praying that Walt would leave his home before Shaw McDonough reached it.

Or he might lose a second father as violently as he'd lost the first. And the woman and child he loved might have to pay too high a price for his careless mistake.

"Sarah?" He made no effort at stealth this time. He stomped up the wooden steps and threw open the front door. "Sarah! It's me. Come on out."

"Coop?" She burst from the closet, her gun safely down at her side. She ran straight to him, clutched at the front of his jacket and quickly backed ahead of him as he walked straight into the bedroom. "What was that? What's happened?"

Coop squeezed her hand before pulling it away and turning her toward the bed. "Put your shoes back on and grab your coat."

They'd already been sleeping in their clothes, so they'd be ready for a quick bug out just like this one.

Sarah quickly tied on her shoes and slipped the denim jacket she'd borrowed from Walt over her sweater and blouse. "You scare me when you don't talk, Coop. What's going on?"

"That was the caretaker with a message from Walt. Grab some of the water and food, in case you get hungry."

She ran off to the kitchen while he returned the Smith & Wesson to his ankle holster, and filled his pockets with spare rounds for both weapons.

He picked up his phone from the bedside table and risked turning it on, just in case this panic was based on a big damn lie. *No Signal.* "Thank God."

Kenny hadn't lied. But Coop could have just as easily muttered a curse. *No Signal* meant there was no way to warn Walt, either.

When he spun around to get Sarah, she was already there, blocking his path. She had a backpack over one shoulder and a refuse-to-budge message on the tilt of her mouth. "Where are we going?"

He'd thank her later for jumping into action just when he needed her to. For now, he turned her toward the door and headed for the shed and truck parked there. "We need to get someplace where we can make a call."

"Because...?" She hurried into double-time beside him.

"Because McDonough's closer on our tail than I thought. And my uncle may have already paid the price."

WALT SAID TO MEET HIM HERE. Down by the old mule barn inside."

"A mule barn inside a mine?"

"Back in the day, that's how the miners pulled their carts. I suppose it was easier to feed and rest them there in the natural shelter beneath the ground."

Sarah held tightly to Cooper's hand as he led her down a long incline toward the flooded lead mine at Bonne Terre, Missouri, halfway between Walt's bed-and-breakfast and the cabin where they'd been staying. Walt and Coop apparently knew their way around the mine, which had been abandoned when rising ground water flooded the deep excavation site. Its exploration had been part of Walt's geology research, and Coop had tagged along on one of those summer visits.

"And he's sure that my dad is the man who called him? How could he get Walt's number?"

Coop had apparently already reasoned out what made no sense to her. "Dumb mistake on my part. Walt's a contact name in my job file. All Austin had to do was look at that file to get a name and address. And, no offense, sweetheart, but I have a feeling your dad took some kind of payoff and has been talking to McDonough. Feeding him information about you and me. So I imagine he's motivated to break into my apartment or police files, or borrow a password from your mom or Seth. Whatever it takes to get the information a man like McDonough needs to carry out his assignments."

Sarah stumbled on the gravel beneath her feet, but it wasn't clumsiness that made her miss a step. "No offense taken. The truth's the truth. My dad is one of the bad guys. Only I didn't want to see it until it was too late."

Coop glanced over his shoulder, adjusted his grip to balance her, and then continued their descent along the old service road down to the blocked-off mine entrance. As far as she could tell, they were alone. There'd been no vehicles in the visitor-center parking lot, no traffic on the road leading here. No one behind them or ahead at the chained-up gate.

He didn't stop until they reached an overhang that had been carved straight out of the gray rock that formed these hills. Sarah shivered as they left the direct rays of the sun and the temperature dropped a good ten degrees.

She'd almost forgotten what she'd said aloud until Coop pulled her into the shadows beside him and asked, "What do you mean, too late?"

Sarah tried to make light of her father's betrayals time and again—stealing money, asking favors and, finally, giving her to Teddy Wolfe. "My dad would sell his soul to feed his gambling addiction. I used to try to forgive him. I tried to understand that he was sick. Maybe I was even an enabler for his addiction." She peered through the bars of the gate along with Coop, trying to see whatever he might be searching for in the underground shadows and the black pit of the mine farther on. "You want to know why I slept with Teddy?"

Coop flinched beside her. "Not particularly."

She wanted to touch him, to reassure him. But he was so tense, so on guard, so uncharacteristically distant, that touching didn't seem to be a good idea at the moment. "My dad owed Teddy money. Two-hundred-and-sixty grand."

Coop swore. "Don't say this." He turned and looked down at her. Blue eyes locked onto green. There was no distance between them now. "He didn't…? Teddy didn't…?"

"He didn't rape me if that's what you're asking." She saw the white of his knuckles where he gripped the bars. How could she tell him she'd been a willing participant up until the moment she'd learned the truth? How could she let her mistake hurt Coop again and again?

"Tell me," he demanded. "Tell me the rest."

The truth was the very least she owed Coop. "When Dad set me up with Teddy, I thought it was a real date, and, yes, we got carried away. But Teddy made it very clear afterward that my dad's debt had been paid in full. That that was all he thought sleeping with me amounted to."

"Your own father?"

The temperature seemed to keep dropping. Her smile was forced. "My own dad. So you see, I don't sleep around. I never have. I'm just stupid—naive—about men."

"Don't say that."

His white knuckles blurred behind a veil of tears. "If they're ten years old, I can handle them just fine. But the grown-up version—I make mistakes. I care when I shouldn't, and I want what I can't—"

Coop's fingers tangled in her hair and his mouth closed down hard, possessively, over hers. His tongue thrust between her lips, claiming her with his taste and touch. Then just as quickly, he drew away.

Sarah's eyes and thoughts had cleared. She had nothing but deep, true blue to look at now. "What was that for?"

"Don't ever mistake being hurt or being used for being weak. Don't believe that giving a damn about someone only sets you up to be some kind of victim." His strong fingers massaged her nape. "There are bastards out there in the world, Sarah. It's that simple. It's why my father was a Marine. It's why I'm a cop. And your brother and mom. It's why you reported Dawn Kingsley's murder to the police—even after what Teddy and your father did to you. You could have walked away and never had to risk your life or be a part of this crap we're running from now. But you didn't. You are the toughest broad I know. And I…"

Sarah heard the same rattle of sound from inside the mine. "What was that?" She looked down at the thick chain padlocked around the iron gate. "Is there another entrance? Do you think we beat your uncle here?"

"It's possible." Coop debated something for a moment. "But he would have to walk the entire length of the mine to get to the mule barn. And the power's not on to light the walkways or boats."

"Boats?"

"It's a big mine. Full of natural caverns that were gutted by miners. In some places the water's only two feet deep, but in others it's two stories deep."

"Wow."

"Wow is right. That was probably just a bat or a rock

falling." He looked back up the slope toward the sunlight. "I don't like being out in the open like this. When Walt gets here, he'll know where to find us."

"And then we can implement Plan B and get all three of us to someplace safe."

"Right." Coop pushed her back behind him and pulled out his gun. "Shield your eyes."

One gunshot later, the lock was toast and they were unwinding the chain and pulling open the gates.

"Come on." Flashlights in hand, he led her into the mine.

He wrapped an arm around her shoulders and rubbed some warmth into her when she shivered. "It must be forty degrees in here."

"And the water's even chillier. This way." The water lapped in the shallow pool beneath their feet as Coop led her across an iron footbridge to a row of stables, painted white and looking relatively new in the dim glow of the security lamps and their flashlights.

Sarah knew a moment of shock. "They don't still keep the animals down here, do they?"

"Nah. The place is being restored as a historic landmark. We'll wait over here."

Reluctantly fascinated by the height and breadth of the cutout stone around her, Sarah glanced from side to side, top to bottom. She saw where a narrow train track split into two—one track curved away into a black tunnel, and the other dropped down a slope and disappeared beneath the surface of the water. She saw a rusted old car, with the handles of tools poking up over its edge, on another track. There were modern conduits to run electricity into the tunnels and up around the cavern arches—part of the restoration, no doubt. She even saw one of the rowboats Coop had mentioned, tied to a rock pillar. Her students would love to come here for a field trip.

But they weren't the first tourists to view the place. "Coop?" She pointed her light down toward the footprints in the loose dirt beneath her feet. "Would these be as well-preserved as the rest of the mine?"

Coop stooped to inspect the tracks. She felt the tension in the air shift, even before Coop pushed to his feet.

"Not unless those twentieth-century miners wore shoes with treads on them."

"You mean like running shoes?"

"I mean like we're getting out of here. Now."

A stall door swung open. Walt Bellamy's shock of white hair gleamed in the shadows before he fell to the ground.

She heard the first crack of a gunshot even before she had a chance to scream.

Cooper cursed. He wrapped his body around hers and threw her to the ground.

Even without her flashlight, she could identify the sticky warmth seeping between her fingers as she clutched Coop's sleeve.

"Oh, my God. You've been shot."

"Screw that. We need to move."

The bullets pinged off the rock. Splatted in the earth.

Coop was crawling, low to the ground, dragging her away from the spray of gunfire.

Was Walt Bellamy dead? Had McDonough found them? How could one man fire so many bullets?

"Can you swim?" Coop's voice was a ragged whisper against her ear.

"Yes."

He wrapped his arms around her and rolled. They tumbled over the lip of the pit and plunged into the icy water below.

Chapter Eleven

The icy temperature of the water was an immediate shock to Sarah's system. She was vaguely aware of sinking into the darkness, of ghostly images of mine cars and elevator shafts rusting for all eternity in the fading illumination of her flashlight.

But then she felt the tug of Cooper's hand at her collar. And suddenly, the need to breathe, to swim, to survive, shot adrenaline to her drowsy limbs and she kicked. Alongside Coop she stroked and kicked her way back to the surface.

They surfaced in the shadowy darkness, gasping for breath. She heard running feet. Voices.

"Over here!"

"Stop shooting!"

"You idiot! I wanted her alive!"

"I hit what I aimed for. I shot the cop."

With a silent signal, Coop pointed toward the opposite side of the dark pool. Sarah nodded, took a deep breath and dove beneath the surface to swim across with him.

Her lungs were screaming for oxygen by the time her

fingers touched the slimy hard wall of rock. She surfaced in almost complete darkness. The disorienting sensation had her spinning in circles, desperate to find the wall again. But then she felt Coop's hand on her wrist. He guided her to an ancient iron ladder anchored to the wall and urged her to climb.

Over the chattering of her teeth, she heard the voices again. One British, one deadly, one she didn't recognize and one heartbreakingly familiar.

"Where are they? Can they drown in this?"

"Shut up."

"Spread out and find them."

Sarah forced her stiff muscles to work—one hand over another. One step. Two. Coop's hand on her thigh and his deep, irregular breathing from below kept her moving.

Either her eyes were adjusting to the pitchy darkness, or she was beginning to hallucinate. She saw their destination above her. A rickety-looking catwalk installed to give access to the conduits, lights and air vents that crossed the mine's ceiling.

"Can you reach it?"

She prayed that Coop's hoarse whisper was deliberate, and not the result of blood loss or a more severe injury than he let on. She reached up and wrapped her fingers around the cold metal. "I've got it."

With a boost from Coop and little luck, she swung herself up onto the catwalk. For a moment it swayed, or maybe that was just her balance protesting her precarious perch. She didn't know if it was a blessing or a curse to see nothing but blackness below her and have no idea how high above the rock and water they were. But on her hands and knees, she scooted along, giving Coop plenty of room to climb up behind her.

There were more shouts and curses below them. She heard the sound of the boat knocking against the pillar in the water below. She heard the crank of oars and wondered if they had entered the cave through the other opening Coop had mentioned—and rowed their way across under the ground to avoid being seen from the parking lot or main entrance.

"Search the water."

While Coop and Sarah crawled toward the next ladder, the movement of their pursuers' lights created a strobe effect in the darkness below. She closed her eyes against the dizzying sensation. "You're still back there, right?" she whispered to Coop.

"I've got the best view in the house, babe. But move it."

"There's a ladder!" someone shouted from below.

The beams of light converged on the wall, then rose to the catwalk and chased them.

"Up there!"

Sarah gasped at the explosion of another gunshot.

"Don't fire! It's too dark to aim and I won't have you miss."

"They're getting away."

"Row!"

Cooper's hand branded her bottom and pushed. "Move it, sweet cheeks. I want to be down on the ground and running before they get to the water's edge."

The ladder was in sight.

"I'm so sorry about your uncle. He was such a sweet man."

"Later, Sarah. I'll have to deal with that later."

She nodded, even though he couldn't see. She would have wept, too, if she wasn't filled with the same urgent need to simply move. Act. Live.

"I've got it." She grasped the side of the next ladder in her fist and gave it a quick shake to make sure it was solid. Then she lowered her foot and felt around for the first rung. "I can't find it. Damn. I wish I was taller."

The lights found them.

"Go, babe."

Sarah held on tightly and stepped down. Into nothing. Her grip slipped at the sudden drop. "Coop!"

"Sarah!"

It wasn't Coop's voice screaming her name as she fell.

But it was his big, certain grip around her wrist that caught her. She heard him grunt with pain as she swung out like a pendulum and then swung back and smacked into the wall. He moaned at the strain on his arm, but he held on.

"I'm sorry," she cried. "I'm sorry."

"Shine the light up there!"

The lights blinded at first, then gave her a glimpse of the two missing rungs of the ladder. She stretched out her leg to hook the ladder and missed.

"Hurry, babe," Coop urged.

Hating that she was causing him pain, Sarah grit her teeth and stretched out with every inadequate inch of her. She caught the edge of her ladder with her toe, pulled herself closer until she could catch it behind her knee. Then her fingertips touched, grabbed.

She looked up. Saw the strain on Coop's face. Saw the blood soaking his sleeve. "Let go, sweetheart." She gripped the ladder with both legs now. "I've got it. I'll be safe."

"Keep rowing!" came the order from below.

Coop released her with a mighty breath and collapsed on top of the catwalk. Sarah shimmied down until she found the first secure rung. "C'mon, Coop." *Don't pass out on me. Don't fall. Don't die.*

"Climb." He pulled out his gun, took several deep breaths. What was he doing? "I'll be right behind you."

Sarah hugged the ladder, cringing at the sound of gunshots right above her head.

But then one light went out down below. Then two. There was cursing. More orders. The grind of oars cranking in their oarlocks.

"Go!"

Sarah needed no more encouragement to descend back into the darkness, knowing Cooper was climbing down right behind her. Coop hit the ground at almost the same time she did. He was breathing hard, clutching his arm near his waist. Still, he grabbed her hand and ran.

They splashed through ankle-deep water to a footbridge, where Coop lifted her up. She could see the rectangular light from the mine entrance where they'd first come in, and broke into a run.

But then she heard the splash behind her. She whirled around. "Coop?"

He hadn't made it onto the bridge. His strength was flagging. He'd fallen back into the water.

Sarah jumped off the bridge and waded over to him. He was down on his hands and knees, his face a scary shade of pale.

"Where are you hit?" she asked, smoothing her palm over his head. He must have lost his cap in the water. His skin was like ice.

"Keep moving," he said, unable to follow his own command. "They're coming."

"I'm not leaving without you."

"I've lost too much blood. I can't get my body heat back up. I'm gonna pass out. I'm slowing you down."

She braced an arm beneath his chest and tried to lift him. "I'll help you."

He pushed her away. "Get out of here!" He was going for his gun, crawling toward the approaching boat.

Sarah got up off her butt and grabbed the back of his soggy jacket. "Don't you wimp out on me now, Bellamy!" She tugged. "Get up!" She tugged harder. "We need you!"

He lurched to his feet and stumbled beside her. Sarah hooked his good arm over her shoulders and willingly took his weight. "Now move it!" she ordered, balancing him as best she could and praying his strength wouldn't give out.

"Sarah—"

"You never left me. I am not leaving you."

They waded through the water, falling once. She picked up Coop's gun and helped him to his feet.

"Finally!" The men were docking the boat, scrambling onto dry rock.

"I can take the shot when they get into the light."

"No!"

Sarah turned and fired blindly into the darkness. She heard a yelp and a splash, cursing and shouting. She fired until every bullet was spent. Then she tucked the gun into her pocket and lugged a groggy Cooper out through the gate and up the shallow incline.

She pulled the gate shut and spared precious seconds to wrap the chain around it. The lock wouldn't close, but she hooked it through the chain anyway. It might not stop them, but it would slow them down.

While she closed the gate, Coop had enough presence of mind to reload his gun with a new clip. He handed it to her as he draped his arm around her shoulders and struggled to make the climb with her. His sweet lips were blue, his teeth chattering. "If I pass out, you walk away."

"No—"

"And if they get any closer, you shoot to stop 'em. You shoot to kill."

Sarah had Coop inside the truck and was speeding away by the time the men cleared the gate and came running up the hill. She'd shot at her own father. Shot at men who surely wanted her dead.

But none of that mattered except keeping Coop alive and keeping her baby safe.

Sarah cranked the heat in the truck as Coop's eyes drifted shut. She was lost in the rocky hills of eastern Missouri long before the men who had killed Coop's dear uncle reached their own car on the far side of the mine and tried to pursue them.

THE MOTEL ROOM SARAH RENTED in a small town in the middle of nowhere wasn't fancy, but the place was clean and the heater worked.

After dragging a shivering Coop inside and bolting the door, she ran hot water in the tub and soaked some towels while she went back to the bed and stripped off his clothes. There was much to admire about his sleek, sinewy frame, but Sarah could only see the deep, oozing gash along his upper arm where that first bullet had grazed him. She didn't feel corded muscle or the crisp, nutmeg-colored hair on his chest and legs, but the alarming chill of his pale skin.

He muttered something unintelligible when she covered his torso with the warm towels and prayed he wasn't so far into hypothermia that her efforts to raise his body temp would be a shock to his strong heart. She kissed his forehead and covered him up. In the time it took her to peel off her own clothes and turn the bath into a shower, the tinge of blue had faded from his lips.

"Come on, big guy." She pulled him from the bed and he walked with her into the shower. She turned him into the pelting warmth of the steamy spray, washing his wound with a fresh bar of soap and massaging heat and life back into his body.

Bordering on exhaustion herself, Sarah held on when he finally hugged himself around her and whispered. "I'll be okay."

Not completely convinced that was just brave talk, considering his shaky balance when she leaned him against the shower wall while she shut off the water, Sarah walked him back to bed and tucked him under the covers. Her concern didn't abate when she soaked a needle and thread in alcohol from the first-aid kit she'd slipped into her backpack, and Coop dozed fitfully while she stitched together the worst of his wound.

"Are your shots current, Coop?"

She thought she detected a nod. But he was still so pale. His breathing had evened out, but his rest was still fitful, judging by the murmurs from his lips.

Sarah tightened the towel she wore like a sarong around her and hung up their clothes over the shower rod and towel bars to dry. When Coop's cell phone fell off his belt and clattered to the tile floor, she picked it up and turned it on to see if it would still work. There was a waterlogged bubble beneath the screen, but she could still read the numbers as she scrolled through his address book and found John Kincaid's number. She recognized the prefix as a KCPD number. He probably wasn't at work this late in the evening, but if she couldn't reach him, someone would be there to take a message. She'd keep the call short, just as Coop had mentioned, then turn the phone off so the GPS coordinates couldn't be traced. But she had an officer down, and if she was the only backup available, then they were in serious trouble.

"Kincaid."

Sarah's heart skipped a beat at the deep-pitched clip in his voice. She inhaled a steadying breath. "Captain Kincaid? This is Sarah Cartwright."

"Oh, my God." She heard snapping fingers, the scraping of chairs and footsteps in the background. He wasn't alone. "Where are you? You and Bellamy dropped off the face of the planet. KCI reported that Theodore Wolfe and two of his colleagues got off a plane in Kansas City yesterday. And then we lost contact. Are you all right? Where's Bellamy?"

Theodore Wolfe and two colleagues. That would explain the voices she hadn't recognized down in the mine. "I want to double-check the correct way to doctor a gunshot wound."

Kincaid cursed. Sarah briefly recapped the events of the past two days, including their run-in with Wolfe and McDonough and her father. Kincaid gave her medical information and promised to check on Walt Bellamy in the flooded lead mine. And though she could read off the name of the motel, she couldn't remember the town they were in. Maybe something inside her didn't want to share that exact information.

Kincaid snapped his fingers again. Apparently, members of his task force were on hand and ready to assist. "Sandoval. Get on the horn. I need the state police to provide backup ASAP."

Sarah hung up and turned off the phone, feeling marginally more secure with the promise of a man Coop so obviously liked and respected.

Finally, after eating an energy bar and brushing her teeth, Sarah checked her patient one more time. His temperature had come up. There was no fresh blood seeping through the gauze over his wound.

But Sarah couldn't rest, knowing he'd been so hurt, feeling he was still so far away from her. So she stripped off her towel and climbed into bed with him.

She snuggled her naked body up against his, offering

him her warmth, offering him the tender shelter of her heart—just as he had shared his warmth and caring with her that night at the bed-and-breakfast, when she'd been just as vulnerable as he was now.

Sarah kissed his jaw and rested her head on the pillow of his shoulder. "I love you, Coop," she whispered into the darkness while he slept. "We both do."

COOP AWOKE TO THE MOST delicious warmth, reluctantly stirring himself from a shamelessly erotic dream.

Oh, but the reality of those drowsy green eyes looking up from beneath his chin was so much better than any dream. He'd been so far out of it, healing his body, resting his brain. But he was back, waking with the dawn outside his window, covered with a bedspread and a naked woman.

Oh, yeah, reality was so much better than anything he could dream up.

"Good morning, sleepyhead."

Hadn't he wakened her, just like this, not so many mornings ago?

"Good morning yourself." His throat was dry, his right shoulder achy. But there were parts of him that felt very, very good this morning.

Sarah tucked her hair behind her ears and propped herself up on her elbows beside him. "How are you feeling?"

A smooth thigh brushed across his and Cooper tensed, hiding his body's involuntary reaction to the innocent caress. "I choose not to answer on the grounds that I might incriminate myself."

But that pretty mouth frowned. "I'm serious, Coop.

Your arm? I fixed it up the best I could. And hypothermia? I didn't think you were ever going to stop shivering."

He pressed a thumb to the corner of her mouth and coaxed a smile. "I'm fine, sweetheart. Thanks to you. I told you you were one tough broad."

"I didn't want to leave you in that mine. I was afraid…" She flattened her palm over the skin atop his beating heart, as if she needed the reassurance that he was still very much alive. "They kept saying they didn't want to shoot me. But they had no problem with killing you. I, however, have a big problem with that."

Great. He'd passed out, hadn't he? Or nearly so. His hands began a roaming exploration of her body, checking for fresh scrapes and sore spots. "Are you okay?"

She tried to catch his hands, tried to stop his search. "I'm fine. I just needed some sleep."

"And the baby?"

"She's not complaining, either."

Giving himself permission to relax for a moment, Coop dropped his head back onto the pillow. "Where are we?"

"To be honest, I don't remember the name of the town. I was more interested in finding a hot shower and a place to sleep. But I figure we're about twenty miles south and west of the mine. I drove for about half an hour."

"Did you use a credit card to register?"

"I paid cash. We're registered as Mr. and Mrs. Ford. From the truck. It was the first thing I could think of. He didn't ask for ID."

Coop nodded. "Nowheresville is good. Anonymity is good." He absently stroked his fingers up and down Sarah's spine, squeezing his eyes shut. The nightmare from the mine blipped into his brain like snatches from a movie. "Walt's dead, isn't he?"

"I'm not sure. Probably. I talked to Captain Kincaid briefly last night. He said he'd send men to check the mine. Oh, Coop, I'm so sorry for ever getting you into this. I'm so sorry."

"Don't." He slipped his fingers up beneath the weight of her hair and cradled her neck. He realized his other hand still rested with a possessive rightness on the curve of her sweet, smooth bottom. And if he wasn't mistaken, that was a breast pressed to his side. And her leg was still wedged with a dangerous bit of innocent abandon between his thighs. "Don't ever blame yourself for anything Wolfe and McDonough have done. I'll shoot the bastard myself for taking that good man from the world. But it's not your fault."

She nodded, then licked her lips in a brave attempt to smile. "I know. But I'll still miss him. I know you will, too."

Coop was mesmerized by the flick of her tongue. By the warmth of her body. By the bravery in her heart and the compassion in her soul.

He combed his fingers through her hair, sifting the silky weight of it between his fingers before drawing her mouth down to his. Her lips blossomed beneath his kiss, welcoming him, wanting him. An answering hunger sparked deep inside him, taking root and sending tendrils of desire into every part of him. He moved his hands to her hips to lift her fully on top of him, needing the soft heat of her body to soothe the sharp need already spiking through his.

Coop wasn't sure when the first tear leaked from the

corner of his eye, but Sarah noticed. She caught the tear with a gentle stroke of her finger, then touched the spot with a healing kiss.

"Oh, Coop," she whispered, catching the next tear. And the next. "It's okay, sweetheart. We'll be okay."

Sweetheart?

The endearment fired something in his brain—a need to be cared for, to be wanted—desired—as deeply as he wanted, no, needed her.

"Sarah." His voice was a husky plea against her throat. His thigh was rubbing between hers, teasing at the smoldering heat there. He slipped his hands between their bodies, catching the tips of her breasts with his thumbs, taunting them until they pearled against him, tempting himself with the need to do more than touch.

"Sarah." He repeated her name like a caress, rubbing his cheek against the soft swell of one breast. "I need you." He squeezed her bottom and held her against his growing arousal, wanting her to be absolutely certain that she knew what he was asking. "Tell me no and I'll go get into the shower. I don't want you to think that you owe me. I don't want you to think this is any kind of debt."

"You're not going anywhere, Cooper Bellamy." She swept her hands over his goofy head and linked her fingers behind his neck. "Not tonight." Her knees separated and slid to either side of his thighs in a bold, welcoming move. "I need you, too."

He rose up to meet her when her mouth descended toward his. He kissed her long and deeply, taking his own sweet time to sample her taste, her heat. The dimple at her top lip, the fullness of the other. He kissed her and kissed her until she was moaning in her throat and squirming with a delicious friction on top of him.

Her needy response fueled Coop's own hunger. If ever he'd considered himself half a man because of his surgery, her eager, indulgent responses shattered that fallacy. He lifted her, dragged her up along his chest until he could claim one sweet morsel of a breast in his mouth. Small, but firm, with eager, responsive tips. He drew his tongue across the distended peak. She gasped his name, clutched the pillow at either side of his head and squeezed her knees around his hips.

"I need you, Sarah." He needed to bury himself inside her. Find a balm for his grief, respite from his fears, a celebration of safety and loving and surviving.

"It's all right, Coop." Her hands slid down to capture his jaw and guide his mouth back to hers. "Hurry." The demands she made were convincing enough. "I don't think I can wait."

Ignoring the twinge in his shoulder, Coop rolled over on the bed, tucking Sarah beneath. He propped himself up on his elbows, loving the teasing way she nipped at his chin, the greedy way she ran her hands down his flanks and grabbed his butt.

He noticed a fullness to her tummy that wasn't there before. Extra curves on her beautiful figure. He tried to talk, tried to do the right thing. "What about the baby? I don't want to hurt her."

Sarah's green eyes were luminous stars as she looked up at him. "You won't hurt her, Coop. I promise. You could never hurt either one of us."

It was reassurance enough. He entered her slowly,

watched the blush color her cheeks and the desire fill her eyes.

He retreated just as slowly, holding himself back, being careful not to crush her in any way. "You tell me if anything—"

The fingers on his bottom clenched. She tilted her mouth for a kiss. "Now."

She lifted her hips and he entered her again, humbled and aroused by her fierce demands. They quickly found a rhythm that matched the seduction of their kiss. And when Sarah cried out his name and pulsed around him, Coop's own need erupted and spilled into her welcoming warmth.

When their passion was completely spent, Coop rolled onto his side and pulled Sarah into his arms. She quickly dozed off, and he smiled into the spicy scent of cheap hotel soap that clung to her hair.

This was almost better than sleeping with sexy Sarah Cartwright, he mused, as his own eyelids grew heavy. Actually *sleeping* with Sarah, when she snuggled into the curve of his body and he could hold her and the precious life she carried inside.

Coop nodded off to sleep, thinking this was right. This was the way it should be between them.

A guy could get used to this kind of closeness.

He already had.

Chapter Twelve

Sarah's clothes were stiff as she hurried inside the gas station to buy herself a late-morning snack while Coop gassed up the truck. She didn't mind the scratchy discomfort, though. She was alive. Her baby was safe. And she was with Coop.

The plan was to get into the truck and drive back toward Kansas City, spending a few nights in various small towns that a foreigner like Shaw McDonough would have a hard time finding and an even harder time mixing in with the locals if he should happen to track them. Coop's goal was to maintain an ultra-low profile but also position himself closer to his potential backup from KCPD. He was still being a grumpy butt about nearly passing out from blood loss and hypothermia and not being able to protect her down in the mine, where the arrangement to meet his uncle had been an obvious setup. But she assured him that his timing had never been better, and that there was no one she could count on more to keep her and her baby safe.

She'd finally figured out that Potosi was the name of the little town and that it was filled with about 3,000 friendly people. Or maybe she was just in the mood to give everyone she met the benefit of the doubt this morning. After all they'd been through together—after making love this morning with a clear intent and regretting nothing afterward—Sarah knew that she really did love Cooper Bellamy.

And as soon as Shaw McDonough was behind bars and they had a chance at a normal life, she would tell him so.

Sarah scoured the snack stands for something relatively healthy, and finally picked up some cheese and crackers and a couple bottles of water. A horn blared outside, capturing her attention along with the other customers in the station. She looked out the window, her heart pumping a little faster when she didn't immediately see Coop at the truck.

She hurried over to the window. When he popped up from behind the back wheel with an air hose in his hand, she breathed a sigh of relief. Nothing was wrong. She looked around the station. The five or six other people inside the store would have reacted as well if something had been amiss.

With a wave to Coop and an answering nod, she took her items over to the cash register and set them on the counter. On impulse, she picked out one of the caps on display by the register. Coop would look good in St. Louis Rams blue. And he'd lost his last cap somewhere in the mine. Sarah grinned mischievously. *A guy could get a sunburn.*

"Put this on the tab, too."

The cashier rang up her purchases. Sarah gathered her items and change and turned to look right into the cold black eyes of pure evil.

She gasped at the cruel nudge of Shaw McDonough's gun at her stomach. Automatically, she hugged her sack between them. When she started to glance to the left, the gun nudged closer.

"Don't look at him.".

Sarah forced herself to look straight ahead at the pink scars on his chin. "What do you—?"

"Say one more word, Miss Cartwright, and I will blow up your boyfriend's truck." She looked down at the tiny remote-control device he pulled from the pocket of his hunting jacket—a simple disguise that helped him blend in with strangers easily enough. "I stuck the explosive under his truck while he was turned the other way. Now leave your things on the counter and walk out the back door with me."

Fearing for Coop, for her baby—fearing for herself— Sarah turned and set the bottles and snacks on the counter. Then she pushed them aside and set the cap in the middle by itself, turning the bill toward the back door.

"Let's go."

Sarah obeyed the prompt of the gun even as her mind spun with ways to get Coop's attention without getting either one of them killed. Her stomach was a tight twist of fear inside her. What could she do? What could she do?

She only caught a glimpse of the fist that hit her the moment she stepped off the station's back stoop.

She crumpled to the ground as pain exploded across her jaw and through her skull. Then, in a woozy bit of observation, the man who'd hit her picked her up and loaded her into the backseat of a waiting car. The man and Shaw McDonough quickly climbed in behind her.

As she collapsed into the corner by the door, she was aware of three things: They were driving away without anyone stopping them.

"Sarah? I asked you not to hurt her." She knew that voice from inside the car, hated the sound of it.

And as they pulled out into the street, Shaw McDonough pressed the trigger, anyway.

"SARAH?"

Coop walked into the gas station. He understood about waiting in line. He understood about women and bathrooms—well, sort of. And he definitely understood about pregnant women and bathrooms.

But Sarah's trip inside the station was taking way too long. Even for a pregnant woman who had to wait in line for the bathroom.

Joke though he might, Coop's senses went on full alert. Something was wrong. Something was off.

He approached the older woman standing behind the counter. "Did you see a short blond woman in here? It couldn't have been more than a couple of minutes ago."

"Sure. She bought some food and a...cap." The woman hesitated as she caught sight of the dark blue cap sitting in the middle of her counter. She pointed to the paper sack beside it. "These are her things. But I don't know where she went."

Coop slapped his hand down on the cap when the woman would have moved it. *No. It couldn't be.* He trailed his gaze along the direction the cap was pointing. Straight to the back door.

No. Hell, no. Coop felt sick to his stomach. Sicker

than he'd been yesterday in the mine when his body was shutting down and his brain was passing out. Where was Sarah?

He picked up the cap and plunked it on his head as he jogged to the back door, already reaching beneath his jacket for his gun.

And the world behind him exploded.

SARAH CAME TO ON THE SOFA in a swanky hotel room, feeling far woozier than any punch in the jaw should merit. As her eyes began to focus in the room's dim light, she could see she had bruises and tape marks and a puncture wound on the back of her left hand, as though she'd had an I.V. stuck there. "What the hell?"

"She's waking up."

A big hand smoothed the hair away from her forehead. And if she squinted hard enough, she could make out the lights of the Kansas City skyline, shining against the black canopy of night. Black, like the pit of that flooded lead mine. Black, like the eyes of…

"Welcome back, Miss Cartwright." Her gaze snapped to the voice of a black-haired man sitting not five feet from her in a plush hotel chair. But the quick action hurt and made her stomach tumble. She closed her eyes and listened. "I'm Theodore Wolfe. I don't believe we've had the pleasure yet. You already know my colleague, Mr. McDonough."

Oh, my God. Her hands flew to her stomach. She hadn't been shot. Her baby was safe. She wasn't dead.

She forced her eyes open, cringing as she realized a man was cradling her head in his lap. "Coop?"

But, no. His truck had exploded. Her heart twisted up in pain at the memory.

Theodore Wolfe was talking again. "And this distinguished gentleman is Dr. Hamad Rajiv. I asked him to run a test on you."

"What kind of test? Where am I? What happened to Coop?"

"Relax, sweetie. I made sure that no one hurt you. I was by your side the entire time." Sarah gagged at the voice of the man on the sofa with her.

She sat up, clutching her swirling head as she scooted to the far side of the couch. "Dad." She ignored him as being of little consequence in her life and turned her attention back to Theodore Wolfe—an older, more lethal-looking version of his playboy son. "What test?"

"To find out if you're carrying my grandchild."

"IF YOU REALLY LOVED ME, if you really wanted to take care of me for a change, you'd help me get out of this place." Sarah glared at her father. The user. The traitor. Wolfe and McDonough and their giant thug of a henchman had locked her in the bedroom with Austin Cartwright while they waited for Dr. Rajiv's test results.

"Sweetie, I did what I could to protect you."

"Bull." Sarah whirled around, desperately hungry and ready to pee. But there was no need stronger than the need to strike back at the man who was ultimately responsible for putting her in this position. "Am I supposed to be grateful to you for pimping me out to Teddy Wolfe? For robbing me of confidence in my own judgment? Am I supposed to thank you for telling

Kansas City's most wanted mobster that I'm pregnant with his grandchild? Did you tell them where I was hiding? Did you stand by and do nothing while a good man was murdered? The man I love may be dead. Am I supposed to thank you for that?"

Austin stood, patting the air in a futile effort to placate her as she advanced on him. "If I hadn't told Theodore Wolfe about the baby, then you'd be dead. He called off the hit on you because I made that phone call."

"This is your grandchild, too." She cradled her stomach, trying to convey a love to her child that her own father had forgotten how to give. "How much did you sell her for?"

He hesitated long enough for Sarah to know it was true. When he'd needed money to feed his habit, he'd used her. And now he'd used her baby, too.

She was done with forgiving. She was too tired to maintain her anger. About the only thing she had left was pity.

Sarah pointed to the door. "There's a murderer out in that room—maybe more than one—and I guarantee you, Dad, that when you're done being useful to them, they'll kill you, too."

He shook his head, tried to reach out to her. *As if.*

Sarah stalked to the far side of the room.

"I love you, sweetie."

"You don't know how." She hugged her arms around her middle, around the place where they'd violated her baby's slumber. She missed Coop desperately, and wondered—prayed—that he might have one more miraculous piece of timing in him. *Oh, hell.* She just prayed he was still alive. She sniffed back her tears, refusing to cry in front of Austin Cartwright, refusing to be the victim of his machinations ever again. "If you were any kind of father, you'd stand up to Theodore Wolfe. You'd leave that door unlocked and at least give me a chance to fight for my own life, for my baby's life. Hell, at the very least, you'd give me a phone so I could call for help."

Sarah waited in silence, refusing to face her father. She heard the door open and close behind her, heard the key turn in the lock.

Her laugh was anything but amused as she turned and glared at her posh prison door.

But then the laughter stopped. Her knees nearly buckled with shame. With hope.

Her father had set his cell phone on the desk beside the door.

MICKEY SANDOVAL WOULD HAVE been a dead man if two uniformed officers weren't already escorting his hand-cuffed ass down to lockup.

Cooper paced the floor of John Kincaid's office, praying for some kind of break that would lead them to Sarah. Hell, praying that she was still alive. It felt good to be back in K.C. Good to be surrounded by as many task force members as Kincaid could rouse in the middle of the night.

But he could never feel truly good or whole again unless he had Sarah Cartwright in his arms and could kiss her senseless.

His uncle was dead. Innocent bystanders had been

injured in Shaw McDonough's latest explosion in Potosi. And Sarah was gone. She'd fight like hell for herself and her baby. If she could. If she wasn't hurt. If she was still alive.

"I can't believe I didn't see what Sandoval was doing. Right under my nose." Captain Kincaid was probably tired of seeing Coop pace. "He's been my gofer on this task force. My right-hand man in a lot of ways. Hell, I was thinking of promoting the bastard."

When Coop had stormed the precinct, loaded for bear after a speedy car ride across I-70 that should have taken four hours instead of two and a half, it hadn't required too much of playing bad cop to ferret out Sandoval and help him confess to feeding information to Shaw McDonough. He had willingly drunk the spiked coffee at the safe house to cover the fact that he'd drugged Kincaid's son and supposedly Sarah as well. And he'd been on hand every time Coop had phoned in a report to Kincaid, slowly but surely tracking his movements every step of the way.

"So what's the going rate for selling out a fellow cop?" Coop finally asked.

Kincaid shook his head. "For selling out our entire task force to Wolfe's top enforcer, you mean. All I know so far is that Mickey is building his mama a nice new house. In Puerto Vallarta. We could have nailed McDonough about a half-dozen times if Sandoval hadn't been giving him a heads-up. And with McDonough in custody, I think we could have gotten him to turn on Theodore Wolfe. Then we'd have the whole trifecta out of commission. McDonough. Wolfe. And his son, Teddy."

Coop's partner, Seth, had set the ball in motion, killing Teddy and closing down the casino and its illegal money-laundering operation. Rebecca Page had uncovered evidence to prove Wolfe International was responsible for her father's murder. Sarah had promised to testify. It had fallen to Coop to wrap up the case for all of KCPD. All he had to do was keep Sarah safe.

"Captain!" A sharp knock on Kincaid's office door tore Coop from his self-damning thoughts.

"What is it?"

"It's a 9-1-1 call. They're patching it through to your office."

"I don't answer 9-1-1—"

"It's Sarah Cartwright."

"WELL, MISS CARTWRIGHT…" Theodore Wolfe handed Sarah a printout of the test results.

She skimmed Dr. Rajiv's report. But she didn't know whether to laugh or to cry. "Ironic, isn't it?"

Maybe she was just too exhausted to care anymore.

"Shaw?" The room was suddenly a bustle of packing. "Gather Miss Cartwright and her things. It's time for us to leave."

Maybe justice was the only thing she *could* care about anymore.

She stuffed the paper into her pocket and tipped her chin as McDonough grabbed her by the arm and forced her to stand. "If you're so desperate to have an heir, Mr. Wolfe, then why did you order Shaw to kill Dawn Kingsley?"

The movement across the room stopped. Shaw's grip tightened painfully.

Theodore Wolfe could spare her that much of a response. "Miss Kingsley was after my son's money. She was an idle diversion, a distraction that was keeping him from doing his job properly. She certainly wasn't an appropriate woman to become his wife. He needed to move on."

"But she was pregnant with your grandchild."

Shaw shoved her forward toward the door. "She's just trying to argue her way out of the offer you made her."

"Wait a minute." Sarah's fingers were going numb. But she didn't bat an eye as Theodore Wolfe crossed the room and stood in front of her, trying to gauge her expression. "Are you saying Dawn was pregnant with Teddy's child?"

"Yes. Hello. That's why Shaw killed her. Not because you ordered a hit. But because she was pregnant. He knew that if Teddy had a child, it would redeem your son in your eyes. Shaw didn't want that."

"Shut up." Shaw jerked her arm in its socket.

But Sarah kept talking. "He wants to take over your empire. I was there. I heard him say it. That's why he wants me dead."

"Shut up, you bitch."

"That's enough Shaw." Wolfe nodded toward his hulking bodyguard. "Let her finish. Shaw knew Dawn was pregnant with my grandchild?"

Sarah rubbed the feeling back into her arm the instant the hulk pried Shaw's grip free. "Yes. That's why he wants me dead, too. Not because I saw him kill a woman in cold blood. But because he thinks I'm carrying Teddy's child, too."

"Theodore, don't listen to the—"

"It's Mister Wolfe." With another nod, Shaw was disarmed and kneeling on the carpet. "You knowingly murdered my grandchild?"

He pulled a gun from beneath his jacket and shot Shaw McDonough dead.

"KCPD!" The door cracked and splintered, then all hell broke loose.

Sarah dove for the floor and crawled for cover.

Perfect timing, Coop.

Chapter Thirteen

The Christmas Eve wedding service had gone off without a hitch.

Well, that wasn't exactly true, thought Coop, while he waited for his brand-new wife to return from one of her frequent trips to the bathroom. It had gone on with *two* hitches.

His partner, Seth, had stood at the altar beside him, looking unusually tall, despite leaning on his crutches. Commissioner Cartwright had cried—like a mom, not a cop—as she sat in the front pew and married off both her children.

Coop had to admire Rebecca Page as she walked down the aisle in her clingy white dress. She was fashion-model pretty, smarter than the man she was going to marry, and the very thing that made his overly serious partner smile.

But then a pretty little blonde with an adorable baby bump on her belly had turned the corner at the end of the aisle. And smooth-talking Coop, always ready with a joke, got his tongue twisted up in his mouth. God, how he loved Sarah Cartwright.

Sarah Bellamy.

Coop threw back the covers as the bathroom door opened.

He was smiling now.

His wife climbed into bed beside him and snuggled close in the cocoon of his arms. He'd already made tender, careful love to her to celebrate the start of their honeymoon. But now came the sleeping part, the holding. Now came the bond that had sealed them together from that first morning when she'd been so hurt and broken inside and had turned to him for help.

"What's that cheesy grin for?" she asked, before kissing it away.

He kissed her right back before tucking her beneath his chin and settling down to sleep.

"It's for showing me how much you love me. Time and again."

"That's what your Uncle Walt said I should do. He said that was the only way to get you to believe that the feelings I had for you were real."

"Smart man."

"Smart man," she agreed, pressing her lips to his heart and hugging him tight.

It still hurt to think about the tragedy of Walt's murder. But the woman in his arms had bravely testified to not one but two murders. And now, Shaw McDonough was dead and Theodore Wolfe would spend the rest of his life in a prison cell. Walt's death had been vindicated.

The task force had received commendations and been disbanded, and John Kincaid was being sworn in as the new deputy commissioner of KCPD come January.

"We can hear you thinking down here, Cooper Bellamy. Is everything okay?"

"Everything's perfect. Your brother has finally decided it's okay if I date his sister…"

Sarah laughed, a sound he would never tire of hearing. She turned in his arms and nestled her back against him. "My fourth-graders approve of you, too."

She laced her fingers together with his and pulled them to that most precious part of her body. "And we make miracles together."

He stroked her round belly, loving the baby as much as he loved the mother. But he paused at Sarah's pensive sigh. "What is it, babe?"

"It's crazy to think how we came together. I owe you my life and my heart and my future."

"But?"

"Shaw McDonough wanted me dead because I was carrying Teddy's baby. Theodore Wolfe had me kidnapped because I was carrying Teddy's baby."

"Do you have to keep saying that?"

"But it was Theodore Wolfe who gave me the proof that miracles do happen. You've got some powerful little Coopers, my bald-headed friend." She pulled his fingers to her mouth and kissed each one, then nestled his hand back down over her baby—*their* baby. "This child was yours even without that test, Coop. I want you to know that. This little girl was always yours—in my heart."

* * * * *

Be sure to look for Julie Miller's new
military romance from Harlequin Blaze
AT YOUR COMMAND
coming in January 2008
wherever Harlequin books are sold.

Bailey DelMonico has finally
gotten her life on track, and is
passionate about her recent career
change. Nothing will stand in the way
of her becoming a doctor...that is,
until she's paired with the sharp-tongued
Dr. Ivan Munro.

Watch the sparks fly in

Doctor in
the House

by *USA TODAY* Bestselling Author
Marie Ferrarella

Available September 2007

Intrigued? Read more at
TheNextNovel.com

HARLEQUIN®
Next™

HN88141

**There was only one man for the job—
an impossible-to-resist maverick
she knew she didn't dare fall for.**

MAVERICK
(#1827)

BY *NEW YORK TIMES*
BESTSELLING AUTHOR
JOAN HOHL

"Will You Do It for One Million Dollars?"

Any other time, Tanner Wolfe would have balked at being
hired by a woman. Yet Brianna Stewart was desperate to
engage the infamous bounty hunter. The price was just
high enough to gain Tanner's interest…Brianna's beauty
definitely strong enough to keep it. But he wasn't about
to allow her to tag along on his mission. He worked
alone. Always had. Always would. However, he'd never
confronted a more determined client than Brianna. She
wasn't taking no for an answer—not about anything.

Perhaps a million-dollar bounty was not the only thing
this maverick was about to gain….

Look for MAVERICK

Available October 2007 wherever you buy books.

Visit Silhouette Books at www.eHarlequin.com   SD76824

REQUEST YOUR FREE BOOKS!

2 FREE NOVELS PLUS 2 FREE GIFTS!

HARLEQUIN®

INTRIGUE®

Breathtaking Romantic Suspense

YES! Please send me 2 FREE Harlequin Intrigue® novels and my 2 FREE gifts. After receiving them, if I don't wish to receive any more books, I can return the shipping statement marked "cancel." If I don't cancel, I will receive 6 brand-new novels every month and be billed just $4.24 per book in the U.S., or $4.99 per book in Canada, plus 25¢ shipping and handling per book and applicable taxes, if any*. That's a savings of close to 15% off the cover price! I understand that accepting the 2 free books and gifts places me under no obligation to buy anything. I can always return a shipment and cancel at any time. Even if I never buy another book from Harlequin, the two free books and gifts are mine to keep forever.

182 HDN EEZ7 382 HDN EEZK

Name	(PLEASE PRINT)
Address	Apt. #
City	State/Prov.	Zip/Postal Code

Signature (if under 18, a parent or guardian must sign)

Mail to the **Harlequin Reader Service®:**
IN U.S.A.: P.O. Box 1867, Buffalo, NY 14240-1867
IN CANADA: P.O. Box 609, Fort Erie, Ontario L2A 5X3

Not valid to current Harlequin Intrigue subscribers.

Want to try two free books from another line?
Call 1-800-873-8635 or visit www.morefreebooks.com.

* Terms and prices subject to change without notice. NY residents add applicable sales tax. Canadian residents will be charged applicable provincial taxes and GST. This offer is limited to one order per household. All orders subject to approval. Credit or debit balances in a customer's account(s) may be offset by any other outstanding balance owed by or to the customer. Please allow 4 to 6 weeks for delivery.

Your Privacy: Harlequin is committed to protecting your privacy. Our Privacy Policy is available online at www.eHarlequin.com or upon request from the Reader Service. From time to time we make our lists of customers available to reputable firms who may have a product or service of interest to you. If you would prefer we not share your name and address, please check here. ☐

HI07

ATHENA FORCE

Heart-pounding romance and thrilling adventure.

A deadly masquerade

As an undercover asset for the FBI, mafia princess Sasha Bracciali can deceive and improvise at a moment's notice. But when she's cut off from everything she knows, including her FBI-agent lover, Sasha realizes her deceptions have masked a painful truth: she doesn't know whom to trust. If she doesn't figure it out quickly, her most ambitious charade will also be her last.

Look for

CHARADE
by *Kate Donovan*

Available in October wherever you buy books.

www.eHarlequin.com

AF38974

HARLEQUIN®

Mediterranean N I G H T S™

Sail aboard the luxurious Alexandra's Dream and experience glamour, romance, mystery and revenge!

Coming in October 2007...

AN AFFAIR TO REMEMBER

by

Karen Kendall

When Captain Nikolas Pappas first fell in love with Helena Stamos, he was a penniless deckhand and she was the daughter of a shipping magnate. But he's never forgiven himself for the way he left her—and fifteen years later, he's determined to win her back.

Though the attraction is still there, Helena is hesitant to get involved. Nick left her once...what's to stop him from doing it again?

www.eHarlequin.com

HM38964

Romantic
SUSPENSE

Sparked by Danger, Fueled by Passion.

When evidence is found that Mallory Dawes intends to sell the personal financial information of government employees to "the Russian," OMEGA engages undercover agent Cutter Smith. Tailing her all the way to France, Cutter is fighting a growing attraction to Mallory while at the same time having to determine her connection to "the Russian." Is Mallory really the mouse in this game of cat and mouse?

Look for

Stranded with a Spy

by *USA TODAY* bestselling author

Merline Lovelace

October 2007.

Also available October wherever you buy books:

BULLETPROOF MARRIAGE *(Mission: Impassioned)*
by Karen Whiddon

A HERO'S REDEMPTION *(Haven)* by Suzanne McMinn

TOUCHED BY FIRE by Elizabeth Sinclair

Visit Silhouette Books at www.eHarlequin.com   SRS27553

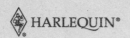
HARLEQUIN®

INTRIGUE®

COMING NEXT MONTH

#1017 RETURN OF THE WARRIOR by Rebecca York
43 Light Street
When the spirit of an ancient warrior takes over Luke McMillan's body, can Luke control his new urges long enough to save Sidney Weston's life—and free this trapped soul, *without dying?*

#1018 HIS NEW NANNY by Carla Cassidy
Amanda Rockport traveled to Louisiana to caretake for Sawyer Bennett's child, not expecting to discover a makeshift family that needed her to hold it together as their secrets pulled them apart.

#1019 TEXAS GUN SMOKE by Joanna Wayne
Four Brothers of Colts Run Cross
Jaclyn McGregor has a traumatic past she no longer remembers. But when ranching baron Bart Collingsworth rescues her from a car accident, he's not buying her story—but it won't stop him from getting mixed up with a woman who truly needs him.

#1020 IN THE DEAD OF NIGHT by Linda Castillo
Chief of Police Nick Tyson isn't the least bit happy to revisit the event that left his own family shattered. But there's no way Nick can turn the other cheek when someone tries to take Sara Douglas's life— even if he hoped he'd never see her again.

#1021 A FATHER'S SACRIFICE by Mallory Kane
Neurosurgeon Dylan Stryker will sacrifice anything, even his own life, to give his toddler son the ability to walk. But it will take FBI agent Natasha Rudolph to face her worst fear to save the man she's falling in love with and the little boy who has already captured her heart.

#1022 ROYAL HEIR by Alice Sharpe
William Chastain and Julia Sheridan lead a desperate hunt to rescue William's son—and restore his royal heritage.

www.eHarlequin.com

HICNM0907